Under Zenith

Shannen Crane Camp

Copyright © 2016 Shannen Crane Camp

All rights reserved.

Published by Sugar Coated Press

ISBN: 1533501610
ISBN-13: 978-1533501615

Cover design by Jackie Hicken
Edited by Jackie Hicken
Photo Credit: Shutterstock

No part of this book may be reproduced or transmitted in any form or by any means, electronic or mechanical, including photocopying, recording, or by any information storage and retrieval system without written permission from the author.

The characters and events portrayed in this book are fictitious. Any similarity to real persons, living or dead, is coincidental and is not intended by the author.

All rights reserved.

DEDICATION

This one is for all of those amazingly imaginative people out there who've made movies, games, books, and everything else that inspired me to write crazy dreamscapes that could only exist in my odd little imagination. And for my mother-in-law who gave me much needed breaks from writing with fudge sundaes, "Once", and drives through the orchards just because we wanted to. And, as always, for The Husband.

Also by Shannen Crane Camp:

Parrish
The Breakup Artist
Pwned
Finding June
Chasing June
Catching June
Keeping June
Sugar Coated
Rose Tinted
Silver Lined

CHAPTER 1

It was a hard dry pill to swallow that all of those sappy love songs had been right all along. You never knew what you had until it was gone. Just like you never really knew how to feel alive until you were already dead.

At least, *I* didn't really know what living was until I had died.

Okay fine, if I'm being fair here I still might not quite know what that felt like since I still hadn't figured out if I was really truly dead or not. You wouldn't think it would be so difficult to know, but apparently it was completely impossible to figure out.

Go figure huh?

But I'm getting ahead of myself a little. Or maybe a lot since I decided to start off this whole thing with the I-think-

I-might-be-dead bomb. But standing on the side of the road looking at my own possibly dead body could shake a girl up a bit.

On the bright side, the night leading up to my sort-of-death had been a really good one. So I had that going for me.

In the end, I think I could chalk it up to one sad fact: I had been killed by *Mumford and Sons* and a dog.

~~~

"Is-la," the hostess called out, completely mispronouncing my name and causing my family to exchange secretive smiles.

"It's Isla," I said, hoping my thick southern accent wasn't preventing me from getting my message across. "Eye-lah," I said again, this time slowly. "You know, like an Island? You don't pronounce the 's'."

"Okay, well your table is ready," the girl continued, just as perky and clueless as ever.

I guess sometimes it just wasn't worth trying to correct people. It wasn't their fault my name was impossible to pronounce correctly when you saw it written down.

It was my mom's fault.

"Thank you, Mama," I called over my shoulder as my
~~~

family and friends followed the hostess to our booth in the restaurant.

"Any time, Sugar," she said with a laugh. "Though I really am sorry they said your name wrong today when you got your diploma. Kind of ruined an important moment didn't it?"

"They even had me write it out phonetically," I exclaimed, feeling very "woe is me" all of a sudden.

My big moment had been thwarted by my impossible name.

"Phonetically? Watch out everyone, college graduate over here is throwing out big words," my brother Tucker said. He draped his arm over my shoulders and ruffled my hair the way only a big brother could.

"Hate to break it to you, but it's not that big of a word, Tuck," I shot back playfully.

"She's got you there son," my dad put in from the back of the group as we all slid into the large corner booth. "And make sure you actually eat something tonight Isla. You're looking like a little stick bug."

"Whose side are you on anyway, Dad?"

"I'm on the side of your sister who worked very hard for four years so that she could end up as a waitress," my dad replied, garnering a dirty look from our hostess.

"Ouch, that was kind of brutal," I said, opening my menu and scanning the plastic page.

"Don't worry Sweetie, there's no pressure on you. We know there's only so much you can do with a vocal studies degree," he said. He gave me a fatherly smile that would have been sweet, had he not been making fun of my education.

They didn't really have room to talk since I was the only one in our family to ever go to college. Sure I'd probably still end up making less money than them, but at least I could say I had a bachelor's degree from East Carolina University, right?

"Don't listen to them, Isla," my roommate Monica said. "You can just move to New York, and suddenly your degree will be like gold."

"Oh don't take advice from the Yank," my dad said. "New York is for people who wear more black than my little girl."

He had a point, I had to admit.

My friends always said I looked like a ghost since I was the only Southerner they knew who was pale. Of course the fact that I had waist length platinum blonde hair and light blue eyes did nothing to help this comparison. I looked like a T-shirt that had been left in the sun too long and had the color bleached out of it.

"Don't worry Hank, I can make her throw out all those white clothes and buy her some black ones," Monica retorted, smiling in my direction and tossing her short dark hair over her shoulder.

"Yeah, that's not gonna happen," I answered with a laugh.

I had a thing for white. With the exception of the "little black dress" every woman was required to have in her closet, and an old pair of blue jeans, most of my clothes were white. I just loved the way a white sundress looked against my pale skin. What could I do?

"I'll bring you to the dark side yet," Monica promised, raising her eyebrows at me knowingly.

"I look forward to it," I responded. I raised my glass of water to her and laughed.

~~~

By the time we finished dinner, it was pouring rain outside.

I shouldn't have been too surprised really since North Carolina seemed to have a bad habit of suddenly opening up the heavens at any given moment and drowning
~~~

everyone in Greenville.

The only thing that *was* unfortunate was my insistence on wearing white. My lacey white sundress was instantly soaked through and I was just grateful that lace didn't exactly become see-through when wet.

That would have been an embarrassing end to the night's festivities.

"Well Baby, we sure are proud of you," my dad said after I'd said goodbye to Monica. My family and I walked through the parking lot, ignoring the rain. "And we got you a little something to show you just how much we respect all your hard work."

"Oh Daddy, you didn't have to get me anything," I said with a smile, secretly hoping they'd gotten me that really expensive leather-bound vocal technique book I'd wanted for so long.

"Your present actually comes in two parts," Tucker said over the din of the downpour.

We all stood in the rain like we didn't even notice that we were soaking wet. We were way too used to the spastic weather here to be bothered by a little flood-inducing downpour.

"Here's the first part," Tucker said, handing over a little flat square wrapped in newspaper.

We definitely weren't fancy when it came to wrapping presents.

I tore the paper off quickly and let out a happy little squeal. It wasn't exactly the expensive vocal book, but I was always grateful for a chance to listen to *Mumford and Sons*. I just loved accents, and I was secretly hoping they'd let me be in their band one day. It never hurt to dream, right?

"Thank you guys," I said honestly, hugging my mom, dad, and brother in turn.

"We haven't even given you the good part yet, Sugar," my mom said with a laugh. "You need something to play that CD in, right?"

"I can just put it on my computer," I said distractedly, turning the CD over to read the titles of the songs.

"Well, just in case you don't feel like listening at home we got you this as well," my dad said, dropping a set of keys into my wet hand.

"Daddy, what is this?" I asked suspiciously.

It was no secret, my family wasn't exactly wealthy. We got along just fine, but I'd had to save up my whole life to go to college, and the little bit of help my parents had given me had come from Mama working two jobs and Daddy saving all he could after house payments and car payments and everything else real life bogged you down with.

So it was pretty much the understatement of the year when I said I was surprised by the brand new red truck my parents were now leading me to.

"You have to be kidding me," I practically shouted. "You guys can't afford this!"

"Oh shut your mouth, we can afford whatever we want if we save for it," my mom said with a little wave of her hand, as if this amazing gift was no big deal.

"Going to college to become a know-it-all doesn't sound so bad now," Tucker teased, poking me in the ribs and grinning.

"Yeah maybe you should try it sometime, Tuck," I said back before turning to my parents. "Thank you so so much! I can't believe you bought me my own truck."

I didn't really know what else to say to them to show how grateful I was, but we weren't really a family of many words anyway so I left it at that. If I tried to expound on my gratitude I'd just end up embarrassing my parents.

"What are you standing around talking to us for? Go test it out!" my dad practically shouted.

He'd never bought a new car for himself. I wasn't sure I could really accept something he didn't even have the luxury of owning so I hesitated, wondering what I should do. There had to be a good way to say you appreciated something without actually accepting the gift, right?

"Baby, if you don't get in that truck right now, I'm gonna give the keys to your good-for-nothing brother," he finally threatened, seeing my reluctance.

I bounced on my heels a few times in excitement before running over and hopping into the beautiful red truck.

It smelled new, the seats felt soft, and the keys in my hand felt like my ticket to an exciting start.

Rolling down the windows before I drove away I blew my parents a kiss, wavy white blonde hair stuck to my wet cheeks.

"I love you guys!" I yelled out the window, excited to start a new life with my bachelor's degree and brand spankin new red truck.

Things from the driver's seat were looking pretty good.

~~~

"A truck?" Monica practically shouted over the phone.

I was driving on the snakelike back roads of town in the pouring rain, feeling like I never wanted to go home
~~~

again. This was just too much fun.

"I can't believe they got you a truck."

"I know," I said back, grinning from ear to ear.

"I guess I don't have to drive you everywhere now, huh?"

"Now I can finally start making it up to you," I replied as I took a corner, my headlights cutting through the rain and the darkness.

"You can start by running to the store to pick up some cat food," she suggested. "Ron Swanson won't shut up. I think he's hungry."

"That dang cat is always hungry. He looks like a school bus with how much we feed him," I replied with a little giggle. "I'll run to the store and pick something up."

"All right. Try not to have too much fun in your fancy new ride."

"Will do, Mon. Bye," I said, my face hurting from the grin that now seemed to be a permanent fixture.

"Bye."

I hung up the phone and tossed it on the seat next to me, taking another corner a little faster than I probably should have.

I could feel the tires skid slightly at the end of the turn but ignored it, finding that the sensation only made me want to drive faster. I almost never got to drive since I didn't have my own car and the feeling was exhilarating. Who knew it could be so much fun?

"I think we need some music," I thought aloud, reaching over for the *Mumford and Sons* CD Tucker had given me.

It was still wrapped in its impossible-to-open CD plastic, so I started tearing at it with my teeth, hoping it wouldn't put up too much of a fight when all I wanted to do was blast "Below My Feet" while driving fast in the best present I had ever gotten.

Beautiful green trees suddenly opened up on either side of me as I crossed over a bridge; the raindrops puncturing the water with little bullets of noise before I was quickly over the bridge and surrounded by trees once more.

I loved Greenville. I knew it was a small town and probably not worth stopping by to most people, but it was where I'd grown up and all I'd ever known. Monica swore that if I went to New York with her I'd never want to leave, but somehow I didn't quite believe her. Besides, people were always sentimental about their own hometowns.

Still trying to tear the CD open, I turned onto another small road, glad that it was so late and no one was out. I didn't want my little joy ride to be slowed down by some ancient tractor lumbering along the road.

"Come on," I said to the CD in frustration, accidentally dropping it under my feet.

Only I was clumsy enough to manage something like that.

"Dang it," I exclaimed in the darkened truck, reaching down to retrieve it.

All I wanted to do was listen to some new music in my new truck. Was that so wrong?

I took my eyes off of the road for just a second, trying to stretch my fingers those last few inches to where I saw the plastic gleaming under foot.

Apparently a second was all it took.

When I glanced back up at the road I could see a little dog standing a few feet ahead of me, looking like it had no intention of moving out of the road. I knew exactly what my dad would do. He'd say the dog shouldn't have been stupid enough to wander into the road to begin with, and he'd let nature take its course.

Normally I'd assume that I'd do the same thing as him. I could be logical and matter-of-fact about death if I needed to be. But apparently my instincts weren't quite as logical as I thought, because before I could even stop to think about it, I was yanking the wheel sharply to the right, trying desperately to avoid the dog that couldn't be any bigger than a chicken.

I felt my stomach drop as the truck suddenly spun around in circles towards one of the big green trees I had found so beautiful only moments before. My hair flew up over my face in slow motion, clouding my vision with long strands of white and I tried to turn the wheel the opposite way to correct my hasty decision.

It was a futile effort as the truck spun out of control, and right before it slammed into the trunk of the large tree I thought, "I can't believe a new truck doesn't have better tires than this."

Maybe I *could* be logical about death.

CHAPTER 2

The mind is a funny thing, and just at that moment, I was grateful for that fact. I couldn't remember actually hitting the tree, just like I couldn't remember crashing through the windshield and landing a good twenty feet away from the truck.

I was almost positive I had buckled my seatbelt before leaving the restaurant that night, but lying face down in the mud with the headlights of my new truck cutting through the space just above me I had to admit, it was looking more and more like I had forgotten.

I used my right arm to roll over onto my back, scared to look down and see what condition I was in. Being thrown from a truck didn't normally bode well for your physical state, and I was sure seeing my white lace dress covered in blood wouldn't do much to settle the panic that I was trying to keep at bay right at that moment.

It took me a full five minutes to gather the strength to prop myself up on my elbows and I let out a little groan at the effort. My body didn't feel broken. It didn't even feel particularly sore. It was just kind of heavy and sluggish, which I guess was pretty good considering what had just happened.

Maybe I would be one of those miracle stories where my belt unlatched itself right upon impact, and I was mercifully thrown from the truck at the exact right moment, causing me to narrowly escape death.

Okay, that might be asking a bit much, but the longer I sat there, feeling like maybe nothing was actually wrong with me, the more it seemed like that was what had happened.

After a little while of sitting in the silent woods letting the rain soak me through, I heard sirens wailing in the distance.

"It's about time," I said, rubbing my forehead where a small headache was beginning to form.

Maybe I had gotten a concussion and that's what was keeping me so calm. That wouldn't be such a bad thing.

The ambulance pulled up quickly, followed by two

police cars, and I couldn't help but think that the neighbors would probably be pretty mad at me for the ruckus I was creating so late at night. I'd have to drop off some brownies or something to apologize for my rudeness.

I could hear the paramedics talking to each other as their flashlights illuminated the inside of my truck, although I couldn't actually make out what they were saying. I knew I should probably get up and walk over to them but my body just felt too heavy. Even sitting up had really taken it out of me, and I couldn't imagine what walking would feel like. So instead I sat there in the mud and the rain, waiting for them to realize no one was in the truck so they could come looking for me.

After a few minutes of them examining the cab of my truck it became obvious that they were aptly distracted by something else and had forgotten the task at hand, since not a single one of them made any move to come find me in the woods. I wasn't sure what was so interesting in there, but they were absolutely fascinated by it.

Sighing and tilting my head from side to side to crack my neck, (something any car accident victim should probably avoid) I slowly and carefully got to my feet, feeling the mud drip off of my dress in thick, heavy clumps. I was just lucky I had worn my brown cowboy boots that night as I slogged through the mud to the sight of the accident.

"Hey Teddy," I said wearily to one of the paramedics who I recognized as a friend of my dad's.

He didn't turn to acknowledge me and I realized that with the rainfall my words had probably been drowned out. I had been kind of quiet.

"Ted, I'm fine, just feeling stupid," I tried again, reaching out to tap his shoulder.

Instead of feeling the scratchy cotton against my hands, however, I was met with nothing but air. It was as if my hand had gone right through him.

I pulled away quickly, startled by the lack of contact and trying to make sense of what had just happened.

"Teddy?" I said again.

Instead of answering me or giving any sign that he had heard me at all, he walked away, returning to the ambulance and grabbing his cell phone from a bag.

"I'm gonna have to call her daddy," he said to another paramedic who nodded at him somberly as he walked away.

"You don't have to call him," I said urgently, thinking about how disappointed he would be when he learned I'd already crashed the amazing new truck he'd gotten me.

Great way to repay your parents, Isla.

Of course Teddy didn't respond since apparently I'd entered *The Twilight Zone* all of a sudden.

"She looks pretty bad," another paramedic said, looking into my empty truck.

"Do you think she'll make it?" the second asked, looking pale as he glanced at the front seat and quickly looked away again, apparently not liking what he saw.

"Hard to say," the first said, frustrating me to no end while other paramedics rushed back and forth between my tuck and the ambulance.

What were they even talking about? I was standing right here, fuming over the fact that they were ignoring me and freaking out because I'd crashed my new truck after only owning it for thirty minutes.

Letting out a frustrated grunt I glanced inside of my truck to see what all the fuss was about and instantly regretted it.

There were just some things you couldn't un-see.

The entire cab was covered in blood, the windshield was cracked, and there I sat with my eyes closed, my once white dress now stained red with my mouth hanging open unattractively.

There was no pale skin to be seen. All I could see was

a sticky red, covering my entire face and a disturbingly deep gash running across my hairline.

“That’s not--,” I began, before letting my words trail off.

I wasn’t sure how to finish that sentence. I had wanted to say that it wasn’t me sitting there, but the evidence was undeniable. It was my body in the driver’s seat of the truck, looking like I’d been dead for a long time despite what the paramedics were saying about a “faint pulse”.

Maybe I’d wanted to say that it wasn’t possible, but the fact that I was looking at my contorted, lifeless face made that argument completely pointless. Why argue about what was possible and what wasn’t when the impossible thing was happening right before your eyes?

“Teddy, did you call her daddy?” the first paramedic called.

“Yeah, I just got off the phone with him,” Teddy answered. “Why?”

“I don’t think she’s going to make it to the hospital,” he said with a sad shake of his head.

“I’m right here,” I yelled, now angry that they couldn’t see me. “You have to hear me, I’m right here.”

I tried shoving one of the men, but my hands went right through them with a little tingle, like sleeping on your arm wrong and losing the feeling in your fingers.

"She's fading pretty fast," the second paramedic said.

"Stop it," I cried, the panic now beginning to take over where the calm had resided only moments before. "I'm right here."

It was quickly becoming obvious that no amount of screaming was going to change the fact that these men couldn't hear me and so, scared and frustrated, I did the only thing I could think of; I ran.

I ran through the mud and the trees as fast as my tingling legs would carry me. I didn't quite know where I was going, but I knew I had to get away from the horrific scene behind me and so I continued to run blindly.

My eyes prickled as if I would cry, but tears didn't come. Instead a sense of dread slowly filled me as my body grew colder and colder in the rain and questions raced through my mind at an alarming rate.

Why couldn't Teddy and the other paramedics hear me? Why couldn't they see me? If my body was at least somewhat alive then what was happening to me now? Was I dying?

I knew I should have stayed behind with my body. If I really was dying I wanted to see my parents one last time. Who knew, maybe when my "faint pulse" stopped, this other version of me would disappear as well and I would have wasted my last moments running away from the inevitable.

The questions continued to circle my mind, the rain continued to fall, and I continued to run until my body couldn't take it anymore and I collapsed in a heap on the forest floor, letting the world around me fade slowly into blackness.

It was the end.

CHAPTER 3

I couldn't be sure how long I had been asleep, but the sun shining in the sky was a good indication that it had been at least a few hours. If I had to guess, I'd say that I had just slept through an entire day and was now starting on the next one, but that probably had something to do with how foggy my mind was.

Images of the truck and my lifeless body flashed through my mind and I tried to block them out as I sat up slowly, taking in my surroundings and thinking that if I still appeared to be in North Carolina, then I probably wasn't dead. After all, I didn't see any clouds or angels with trumpets surrounding me, and unless I had been living in heaven all along, I was still in my hometown.

I couldn't hear the birds I had grown so accustomed to

and the air felt oddly silent, but I definitely had more pressing matters to worry about and so, I ignored this little detail. The only thing I wanted to waste my already overloaded mental space on was what in the world had happened last night.

Crashing my truck was a memory I sadly couldn't erase, this I knew. But what about seeing my own body in the driver's seat? Had I been dreaming? Maybe Monica and I had decided to celebrate after I got home last night and this whole thing was just some crazy dream.

Maybe I was having my own *Hangover* moment, and waking up in the middle of the woods was the end of the story and now I had to retrace my steps to find out what had really happened the night before.

As amusing as this possibility was, I knew it was the least likely scenario for what was going on. Instead of trying to imagine my life as a comedy, I accepted the tragedy it was, stood up and brushed off my spotless white dress (that was suspiciously devoid of any traces of mud), and began walking through the woods.

I wasn't quite sure which way would lead me out of the forested area, but sitting around on my butt wasn't going to get me anywhere so I continued to walk, taking in my surroundings and trying to let my hunting experience come back to me.

Daddy would have been proud that I'd retained anything he'd taught me while hunting, even if it wasn't proving particularly useful at that moment. At the thought of my family, however, I suddenly felt a pang of sadness. If I really had died last night, what would that mean for them? How would they be taking the news? Did they know yet?

This was something I didn't think I was mentally prepared to face and so I continued to walk, keeping with the theory that I hadn't died and I was just in some sort of bizarre dream or the victim of a night of partying.

My body still felt warm and tingly and glancing down at my hands I could see that something was very wrong.

Or very right, considering how great my skin looked.

I'm not talking, I-just-put-some-lotion-on, good. I'm talking, I'm-a-contestant-on-*The-Bachelor*-and-now-my-skin-shimmers-and-glows-like-a-sunrise, good. My skin was still as ridiculously pale as it had always been, but it had a healthy shimmer to it that almost made me look like I was radiating light from the inside out. I bet Monica would *really* think I looked like a ghost now. Skin that heavenly could only come from dying and going to the Other Side.

It was odd that of all the hints I'd gotten that I might, in fact, be dead, the one that really put the nail in the (hopefully hypothetical) coffin for me was flawless skin.

I guess no matter how much Daddy tried to get it out of me, I was still a girl at heart.

It felt like a good two hours that I'd been walking when the sky began to go dark. The sun didn't appear to be setting, but an odd fog had rolled in, dimming the brightness of my surroundings and making it even harder for me to find my way when I was already hopelessly lost.

Greenville had never really been a particularly foggy place, especially not when the sky was completely clear and sunny only moments before, and I wondered if this sudden change in the weather was some sort of confirmation that I wasn't where I thought I was. A light breeze began to blow and my wavy, icy-blond hair tickled my bare shoulders, making me shiver.

The world had quickly gone from a picturesque scene in the southern woods to something resembling *Sleepy Hollow*. The sudden change was unsettling to say the least.

I stopped my aimless walking, knowing I wasn't really being productive by wandering around anyway, and rubbed the goose bumps on my arms.

Something was very wrong with this place. I knew I shouldn't be all that scared of a beautiful forest, but when that beautiful forest mysteriously materializes after you've died, you'd be dumb to not be a little suspicious.

Plus, something about the entire area just felt off. I couldn't get rid of the nervous feeling in my stomach.

A twig snapped a few feet behind me as I stood observing my surroundings and I instantly spun around, worried there might be some sort of wild animal following me.

The truth however, was much more bizarre than a wild animal.

And much more attractive, if I was being honest. I may have been lost and scared but I wasn't dead… well… hopefully.

"Who are you?" I asked the ridiculously good looking man standing behind me.

If I looked like a washed out pale ghost, he looked like my exact opposite. His dark hair, blue eyes, tan skin, stubbly face, and black ensemble resembled something from a 1950s bad boys handbook and I was instantly wary, if not slightly intrigued by this man who had mysteriously appeared out of the fog.

He had a thick black fan of eyelashes lining his icy eyes and I wondered, not for the first time, why boys always had the most gorgeous eyelashes when girls had to work so hard at it. If I had his eyelashes I'd never wear eyeliner or mascara again. Of course boys didn't care at all about that sort of thing which made it even more unfair.

"I'm Hayden," he answered in a thick British accent, his voice impossibly deep.

Okay, if I was dead and *this guy* was my reward for living a good life, I was completely fine with that. Accent and all.

Maybe he wasn't all that good looking, if you weren't into the whole chiseled jaw, sharp cheek bones, and full lips thing. But I could attest that I *was* a fan of those features.

"I'm Isla," I answered with a stupid little smile.

I swear I wasn't some weak-minded girl who fainted at the sight of an attractive man, but my mind had been slightly unraveled ever since the crash so I felt completely justified in the embarrassing little giggle I involuntarily let out.

"Yeah, I'm not an idiot, I know who you are," he replied, lifting his lip into a half sneer and instantly making me take back my thought that he was a reward for my tragic and untimely death.

"Oh," was all I could think of to say.

What were you supposed to say when you were lost, possibly dead, and in the company of someone who wasn't turning out to be as gentlemanly as those British actors would lead you to believe?

Thanks a lot, Hugh Grant.

"Well come on, we don't have all day now do we?" he asked rhetorically, not waiting for my response as he passed by me, leading the way to who knew where.

"I'm sorry, but who are you?" I asked again.

"Hay-den," he said slowly, sounding his name out for me as if I might be dense, and not bothering to turn around or relax his pace.

"I'm not asking your name," I said, letting my indignation take control. Just because I was dead didn't mean this guy was allowed to be condescending to me. My daddy would have had a thing or two to say about his manners right at that moment. "I'm asking *who* you are. There's a difference."

"I don't know if it's the accent or the brain trauma, but something tells me you're not quick on the uptake, are you?" he asked me, managing to insult me yet again.

"Hey!" I yelled, grabbing him by the arm and spinning him around to face me. "Just because I talk slow doesn't mean I'm an idiot," I informed him, wishing I didn't have such a thick Southern accent at that moment. It was apparently not garnering any brownie points with this man and his sophisticated British accent. "Now tell me who you are or I'm not walking another step."

I crossed my arms over my chest and stuck out my chin defiantly. My family hadn't raised a push-over.

The man let out a deep, long-suffering sigh and I could practically see the will power it took for him to keep from rolling his eyes at me.

"All right little girl," he began, though he couldn't have been older than 27. Not really fair grounds for him to call me little at age 21. "I'm your Guide, we only have a few hours to find your first task, and if we want to make *any* progress today we need to move now."

With that sad excuse for an explanation he turned away from me and continued his tromp through the foggy woods, leaving me to jog in an attempt to catch up to his long strides. I couldn't believe I had thought he was attractive. All it took was him opening his mouth once to instantly shoot down that idea.

"You're my Guide?" I asked.

"Yeah," he replied over his shoulder, never once looking back or slowing his pace.

"And what exactly does that mean?"

"It means I guide you," he said in exasperation.

"I know you think I'm an idiot because I don't

understand what's going on right now, but you're doing a horrible job of explaining things to me so really, this is your fault," I said stubbornly, angry at this man who obviously thought he was so much better than me.

My insult got his attention pretty fast. He stopped suddenly and turned to face me once more, causing me to crash right into his chest with the sudden unexpected movement. I stumbled backwards a few paces but quickly regained my footing, feeling like I didn't want to look weak or clumsy in front of this pompous jerk.

"Okay, listen, because I'm only going to explain this once. I'm your Guide. You're stuck here until you get to your Destination, but the only way to do that, is to accomplish a series of tasks. I'll lead you to the tasks, tell you what you need to do, and wait for you to complete them. You'll have one per cycle and once you've completed them all, you'll reach your Destination and I can get rid of you. Got it?" he asked, his voice deep and menacing.

Oh yeah, he was definitely trying to play up the whole bad boy approach. Luckily I could see right through his gruff exterior. I was a Southern woman after all. I wasn't scared of some dainty British man.

"Now you listen to me," I began, my voice firm as I

raised a finger up to his face. "I want answers right this second and if you don't give them to me, I'll just sit here and let you fail as my Guide. I don't know who you work for, but I'm sure failing doesn't look good no matter who your boss is," I said, finally lowering my finger and giving him my best glare.

I wasn't trying to brag or anything, but I had inherited my Mama's glare and it was pretty intimidating.

"Well I can tell you're going to be a handful, aren't you?" he asked, sighing again but not turning around and stomping away like I had expected him to. I guess we were making some progress. "What do you want to know, Princess?"

I ignored the insult in favor of getting the answers I wanted.

"Am I dead?" I asked, starting with the most pressing matter.

"I don't know," he said with a shrug. "Next question."

"What do you mean, 'you don't know'? How do you not know something like that if you're my Guide?"

"You don't even know what a Guide is, so don't start making up a job description for me based on your own irrational fears about what's happening here."

"I just want to know if I'm dead or not," I practically

shouted, fed up with this man already.

"I. Don't. Know," he said again, emphasizing each word. "You could be dead, you could be in a coma. Heck you could be dreaming. All I know is that I need to get you to your Destination so you can move on."

"Move on? To Heaven or something?"

"I'm not sure how many times I can tell you 'I don't know' until it finally sinks in," he said, rubbing his temples in frustration.

"So I might not be dead?"

"I'm really beginning to hope you are," he answered.

"You take that back right now, mister," I said indignantly. "Just because you think you're all superior to me, doesn't mean you get to be rude."

Hayden was silent for a moment, his brooding eyes studying me before he actually let out a small, short-lived laugh that died almost the moment it escaped his lips.

"Okay, fine. I'm sorry I said I wished you were dead. Now do you have any other pointless questions for me or can we get on with things?"

"Can I ask you questions while we walk?" I proposed, still not ready to just blindly follow this person I didn't know. I wasn't a complete idiot.

"I'd rather you didn't," he replied, glancing at me over

his shoulder as he, once again, began his trek. "But somehow I get the feeling there'll be no shutting you up no matter what I say."

"It's a good thing that you're realizing this early on," I said, almost smiling.

He didn't say anything in reply but shook his head in front of me, leading the way through the woods without a word.

"So I may or may not be dead," I began, thinking out loud and trying to sort through things to figure out what in the world was really going on. "But no matter what, I have to get to this 'Destination'," I continued. "So if I'm dead, the Destination is probably Heaven… or something like that, and I'm currently in Limbo."

"You're not a child are you? Isn't Limbo only for children?" he asked, raising a thick dark eyebrow at me and lifting the corner of his mouth.

It made sense that the only time he'd sort of smile would be when he was mocking my intelligence. This man wasn't very hard to figure out.

"I may not be an expert on the Catholic faith, but I think you don't quite fit the requirements for Limbo. Purgatory maybe, but not Limbo."

"I'm not Catholic either but given my current

predicament, maybe I should have been," I said, looking around at the endless expanse of fog and thinking maybe Purgatory wasn't such a bad concept if this was all it was.

Of course being stuck with a rude, British, pseudo-bad-boy was kind of like eternal damnation.

"Okay, so there's the Purgatory explanation," I began again, not bothering to wait for Hayden to make a snarky comment. "There's the possibility that I'm in a coma and my Destination is waking up from that. And then there's the very real possibility that I'm dreaming and my Destination is just waking up in my bed and wondering how I was ever creative enough to imagine a scenario like this."

"I'm so glad we talked through all of that," Hayden said sarcastically. "And what explanation do you think is the most realistic possibility, because I'd really like to avoid starting off every conversation with, 'If I'm dead, or in a coma, or sleeping then why is this happening?'," he said, mimicking my high pitched voice and Southern accent disturbingly well.

I thought his question through for a moment.

This was all too realistic to be a dream. There was always the possibility that the paramedics had stabilized me enough to get me to the hospital where I was currently lying in bed in a coma, but given their assessment of my condition when they'd found me, that seemed like a very optimistic outlook. I wasn't sure there was any way to come back from the amounts of blood I'd seen in my truck.

And that only left me with one other option.

"Hayden?" I asked, my voice small despite my efforts to look tough in front of this stranger.

"What?" he asked, annoyed as usual that I dared to speak to him.

"I think I'm dead."

CHAPTER 4

We walked for a long time through the woods, mostly in silence since Hayden had some sort of aversion to speaking and I didn't really feel like trying to suck up to someone so rude. Instead, I attempted to come to terms with my death. Honestly, I wasn't really as sad for myself as I should have been. I was more worried about my parents.

Like I'd said before, I could be logical about death.

I'd driven recklessly in the rain and I'd died. It was my own fault and I couldn't really get all bent out of shape over the fact that I was now facing the consequences of my own stupid actions. But it wasn't fair that my parents now had to pay for a funeral that they couldn't afford.

Of course I was sad that they would undoubtedly be upset about my passing, but my logical mind could only go right to our financial situation. My parents were good people. They were hardworking and frugal. I always tried to encourage them to splurge a little on a vacation just for the two of them, but they just weren't the spending type.

Now they'd have to spend any potential vacation money on their dead daughter.

Not to mention the smashed truck, the cost of the ambulance, and whatever other charges went with burying a family member. I wished I could visit them in some ghostly form to tell them to just skip the whole funeral thing and just toss my body into the river or something. I didn't need a fancy coffin and loads of flowers that they couldn't afford.

"I hope I'm dead," I said quietly.

"What is it now?" Hayden asked, still sounding as put out about my existence as ever.

"I really hope I'm dead, not just in the hospital or something," I repeated.

"I thought you'd already decided you were dead. Why are we going back on that theory now?"

"I'm not going back on it," I said defensively. "I'm just saying, if I was in a hospital my parents would be racking up quite a bill over me. It would be so much better if I'd just died and all they'd have to worry about is a funeral."

"You're a little morbid," was all he said.

"I'm just being realistic. Judging by what I saw in my truck, I'm not going to live through the accident. If I died right on site it would be better for my parents financially. If I lived long enough to be in the hospital for a few days, then died, my parents would have to worry about the hospital bill *and* the funeral, and that's just not fair to them."

"Maybe you lived through the accident," he stated, not really in a tone that suggested he was giving me hope. It was more like he was trying to kill time with mundane conversation.

"Ugh, that would be even worse."

"How so?" he asked.

"If I lived, my injuries will probably require physical therapy or some sort of medication or… I don't know… something expensive," I said, ticking the possibilities off on my fingers.

"All you think about is money. It's a little disturbing."

"When you're poor, you have to think about money all the time," I told him honestly, wondering if he'd ever been poor enough to worry about money. "What did you do? I mean… before you died. Or have you always been a

Guide?"

"We really don't need to do this," he answered gruffly.

"Do what?"

"The whole 'let's get to know each other because we're stuck together' thing. I'd prefer if we kept this professional."

I gave him a skeptical look, raising one eyebrow and smirking.

"What?" he asked, now taking his turn to sound annoyed at my vague expression.

"How do you keep some sort of weird *Twilight Zone* relationship professional?" I asked.

Whatever was going on here was far from business suits and contracts. It was something straight out of a sci-fi movie.

"By not asking me stupid questions and keeping your mouth shut."

"You're rude and unpleasant and I really don't like you," I told him bluntly.

Maybe it was rude of me to say that to him, but he was definitely asking for it. And really, I probably shouldn't have tried to be nice to him at all. He hadn't really earned my friendship in the least.

"You're the one who got yourself killed. I'm just doing

my job," he stated. "Guess you shouldn't have been such a reckless driver huh?" he asked sarcastically.

"If you must know, I was trying to avoid a dog in the road," I answered primly.

Hayden didn't say anything. Instead he pressed his lips tightly together and smiled, trying to hold in laughter I was assuming.

"What?" I asked in an annoyed tone.

"I could have pegged you for some sort of animal lover," he laughed. "You died because you tried not to hit a dog?"

"That's not funny," I insisted, angry that he was reducing my death to something so insignificant.

"Oh, you're going to love this first task then."

"You keep saying there's a task, but all we've done is walked for hours," I complained. Not that I really had anything to complain about. Somehow, I wasn't tired at all, which I found very odd.

We'd been walking for a good three hours and yet, I felt like it had only been a few minutes. My feet didn't hurt, I wasn't out of breath, and I couldn't even feel myself getting a sunburn through the fog.

"First task: Agility," he said cryptically, stopping his trek near a river.

We were still surrounded by the beautiful North Carolina greenery, though the humidity was surprisingly gone. Something I was very happy about.

See? Purgatory wasn't that bad.

"Agility?" I repeated. "Do you want me to cross the river using the rocks or something?" I asked, still puzzled by the situation.

"You need to get to a cabin about a mile from where we are right now," he said, pointing to some unseen place past the river. "It'll be due west."

"That's it?" I asked.

There was no way the task could really be that easy. It just didn't make sense. What did walking a mile in the woods have to do with agility? I'd already walked several miles with Hayden.

"You'll have some company," he stated simply, leaning against a tree and picking at his fingernails disinterestedly.

"I hope you don't mean you," I said pointedly.

He looked up at me calmly and simply smiled. Unfortunately, his smile creeped me out much more than his cryptic brooding ever could.

I would have asked what he'd meant by his comment, but before I could decipher it, I heard a growl far off in the distance.

"What's that?" I asked.

"Motivation to keep you going quickly. You know? Agility?"

"Is it like some sort of animal?" I asked, suddenly feeling my worry leave me. This really would be easy. "Piece of cake," I told him. "It'll be just like hunting with my daddy."

Hayden gave me an appraising look, maybe trying to figure out if I was bluffing or not. I wasn't quite sure why he cared if I really thought the task was easy. It wasn't like he could do anything about it.

"Well we can't have this being too easy now can we?" he asked. "I guess animals aren't a great motivator for you."

"Sorry," I said smugly, already picking my way across the rocks, managing to get half way across the river without ever getting wet.

I turned back to look at Hayden, wanting to gloat a bit more about how I'd been taught to fashion a bow and arrows from cast off wood lying on the forest floor, when a wolf walked out of the shadows of the forest, right beside him. I felt my heart start a bit at the sight of the animal, but I didn't run. I knew there were so many ways I could take care of it if I needed to, using only the tools I had around me.

One of the rocks in the river could be the end of that wolf and he'd never even know what had happened. I was far from hopeless.

"The cabin is your safe house," Hayden said easily, leaning down and placing a finger between the wolf's eyes gently.

The animal instantly collapsed onto the dirt covered forest floor without a sound. It didn't appear to be in any pain; instead it looked as if the creature had simply stopped living.

"What did you do to it?" I asked, in horror.

Like I said, I was logical about death. I'd been around hunting my entire life. But I'd never seen a human being kill an animal with one touch. There'd been no force involved at all. It was almost as if Hayden had simply sucked the life out of the creature with his finger.

"If you can get to the cabin and lock the door, you will have completed the first task," he went on, not bothering to answer my question.

"Why'd you kill the wolf?" I asked, still balanced precariously on a rock in the middle of the river. "I thought that was my job."

"Your job is to run," he told me simply. "And the wolf didn't scare you enough to do that."

"So you killed it?" I asked, not feeling like his logic really made much sense. "Now I have even less motivation to run."

"I don't think you do."

The wolf's lifeless body began to twitch at Hayden's feet. It moved and contorted in an unnatural way, causing me to shiver. I could see the grey fur quickly becoming brown, then black, then melting off of the corpse all together until all that was left was an off looking pile of skin and bones.

"What are you doing?" I asked Hayden slowly, letting my eyes lock on his and wondering if he really was there to help me.

Something told me that only some sort of darkness could do what he was currently doing.

He gave me a quick wink as the pile of skin began to pull itself up from the ground, revealing something resembling a decaying human form and instantly making me want to vomit.

"I'm motivating you."

CHAPTER 5

"What's that supposed to be? A zombie or something?" I asked with a nervous laugh.

Animals didn't scare me. Being alone in the woods didn't scare me. Even Hayden with his faux bad boy thing didn't scare me. But something about the twitchy movement of the corpse staring at me with its empty eye sockets stirred a primal fear deep within me.

"Sure, we can call it a zombie. I'm sure it wouldn't mind eating your brain," he said with a laugh, apparently finding the whole situation very amusing.

"You watch too many sci-fi movies," I told him, still not running.

Don't get me wrong. I wasn't *that* tough. The zombie-like thing definitely scared me. But it also intrigued me. It was fascinating to see something up close that looked like a special effect in a movie.

"It won't really kill me, will it?"

"You're already dead," Hayden pointed out.

"True," I agreed.

"But that doesn't mean it can't hurt you… a lot."

My eyes widened at this statement, and suddenly I had to wonder what kind of place this was. What was the point of having a zombie chase me through the woods to a cabin? It made absolutely no sense unless you were on the set of a reality TV show.

"Are you going to help me or just stand there and laugh while this thing eats my brain?" I asked him incredulously, wondering if the corpse would make a move to chase me.

Luckily, every zombie movie I'd ever seen suggested that the creature would be a slow moaning mess.

Still, I didn't really have a way to defend myself against it.

I wasn't a naturally queasy girl, but I didn't think I could bring myself to kill something that looked like a human. It just didn't feel right.

"I can't help you, Isla. You have to do this yourself," he said with a shrug, not really sounding like he felt all that bad about this fact. "And I suggest you run."

"Zombies. The great motivator," I joked, keeping my eyes trained on the corpse. "It's just standing there. Why isn't it moving?"

"I think it's trying to be a good sport and give you a head start maybe," he said, looking over at the corpse who, in turn, turned its head with a loud crack to face Hayden.

He shrugged at the thing.

"I say you just get to it, mate," he said.

At first I thought he was talking to me. Then, as the corpse turned to look at me with the black holes where its eyes should have been, I realized he was giving the zombie motivation.

Some Guide.

"I hate you," I said to him as I instantly turned on my heel to finish crossing the river.

One of my boots slipped on a moss covered rock, twisting my ankle and sending me sprawling into the icy cold water. My knees and palms painfully made contact with the rock lined river bottom, and the water forced its way down my throat, rushing over my head for a moment until I pushed myself up.

I turned around to say something my mama wouldn't have approved of to Hayden, when my vision was suddenly blocked by the corpse. I screamed in panic, not expecting it to be so close to me already, and I threw up my arms to defend myself.

Apparently I wasn't as agile as I'd expected because the creature grabbed me by the shoulders and forced me back into the water, hitting my head agonizingly on the rocky bottom and causing stars to spring to life in front of my eyes.

I thrashed against its weight, sputtering for air in the water that was quickly robbing my body of heat. I could feel the bony fingers closing around my throat when I kicked out with my boot, hitting the (for lack of a better word) "zombie" in the place where its stomach should have been.

It released me momentarily, and I took the opportunity to scramble to my hands and knees, crawling out of the water desperately.

"Hayden!" I screamed, looking back over my shoulder to see an empty space where my Guide had once stood.

The creature didn't waste any time getting back to the task at hand, and soon it was crawling out of the water after me at an alarming pace. Really, the sight of a running corpse was all the motivation I needed to get to my feet and run at a full-on sprint in the direction of the cabin with water sloshing in my boots.

So much for slow, moaning movie zombies.

The involuntary dip I'd taken into the river was enough to turn me around, but luckily the sun was setting through the fog and Hayden had so kindly pointed out to me that the cabin was to the west. Still, as I ran towards the setting sun, I didn't know that I'd be able to outrun the creature for a full mile. I was a slow runner and it was quickly gaining on me.

Of course, the cowboy boots in thick mud probably didn't help my situation much.

"Hayden!" I yelled again, hoping this time he'd offer me something more than a few sarcastic comments.

Didn't he care that this thing was trying to kill me?

Okay fine, so I was already dead. But it was definitely trying to hurt me and Hayden was showing a serious lack of chivalry by ignoring that fact. He would *not* make it in the south with an attitude like that.

"Help me!"

"You're getting closer," I could hear him yell far ahead of me.

I wasn't sure how he'd gotten in front of me without my knowledge, but somehow he was already at the cabin. Now I was definitely unimpressed by his manners. He couldn't have just waited for me?

"I don't see the cabin," I yelled into the fog that was quickly growing thicker and thicker.

A cold sensation shot through my arm and I slowed down to grasp my wrist, just for a second.

Big mistake.

I screamed once more as dry, bony fingers clasped my shoulder and pulled me backwards onto the ground. My white blonde hair flew up around my face, clouding my vision and the awful smell of decay instantly hit my nose.

"Help!" I screamed again, kicking out at the creature to keep it at bay.

"I can't," was Hayden's simple reply, much closer than he had been before.

Knowing I was the only one who could get me out of this, I closed my eyes tight, brought my knees up to my chest in a gesture that was very unladylike in the knee length dress I was currently wearing, and kicked with all my might at the corpse that was quickly descending upon me.

I heard a sickening thud as my boot made contact with the creature, but I didn't open my eyes until I heard it hit the ground a few feet away.

"Not bad," Hayden said, now standing over me and

looking amused.

"You were going to… let me die," I sputtered between deep, panicked breaths.

I couldn't seem to stop the hysteria that was building within me.

"Already dead," he said again.

He just loved to point that out to me.

I didn't say anything but stared at him incredulously. How could he be so callous about the whole situation?

Laying my head back against the loamy earth, I closed my eyes and tried to catch my breath again.

"I wouldn't just sit there if I were you," he informed me.

"I just need to rest for a minute. I feel so heavy all of a sudden."

"The longer you're stationary, the more likely it is that more of those things will show up," he stated.

"Great. That's just what I need," I answered with a deep sigh, heaving myself up off of the ground and hoping the cabin wasn't too far off.

Only moments before, I had been amazed by just how much stamina I had; it was like I'd taken some sort of miracle drug. But now, it took all of my will power just to put one foot in front of the other.

“What’s wrong with me, Hayden?” I asked, feeling completely exhausted.

“Wait,” he began gravely. “That zombie didn’t bite you, did it?”

“I don’t think so,” I answered, my eyes wide with fear. “I mean I guess it could have. Why? What does that mean?”

“Nothing,” he replied with a laugh. “Just wanted to scare you.”

“You’re the worst Guide in the world. Are all Guides like this?”

“Like what?”

“Mean and awful to their… people?” I asked, unable to think of a word to describe what I was to him.

“I don’t know. I guess,” he answered distantly.

His eyes were trained on some unseen spot in the distance and I instantly quieted myself, wanting to know what he was focusing on.

“Footsteps,” I whispered.

Hayden nodded, looking at me with raised eyebrows.

“I guess that’s my cue then?”

“I’d say so,” he answered.

“Ugh. I hate being dead,” I told him as I forced myself to resume my run towards the unseen cabin.

My legs still felt as if they were filled with concrete, but anytime I felt like stopping, I'd conjure the image of the zombie attacking me and that motivated me enough to keep going. It wasn't long before I could see the hazy outline of a small structure in the distance, and suddenly I had hope that I might actually make it out of this thing alive.

No pun intended.

As I neared the cabin, Hayden stuck his head out of one of the windows, looking as smug as ever and nodding behind me.

"You should probably watch your back," he called.

I didn't bother looking behind me. I already knew what I'd see. Instead I pumped my arms harder and ran as fast as I possibly could, hearing the crunching of leaves getting closer and closer behind me as I neared the door.

As much as I wanted to deny it, I knew I wasn't going to make it to the cabin door before the creature caught up with me. The only problem was, I wasn't sure what else I could do. It was quickly gaining on me and there was no place to hide.

I knew my brother Tuck would have been able to simply overpower the thing, but he was bigger and stronger than me. It was just like when we were kids and he'd chase me around the yard, trying to "wrestle"; which just meant he wanted to be able to playfully beat me up without getting into trouble. The only defense I'd had against him was the fact that I was small and agile. I could climb trees like a squirrel.

Glancing over my shoulder for just a second, I wondered if the corpse would be able to climb a tree without any muscles. It was certainly doing a good job of running without muscles, so it was very likely the thing could follow me right up a tree, though at that particular point in time, I didn't really have many other options.

It was either climb a tree and maybe get attacked by a reanimated corpse, or keep running to the cabin and definitely get attacked.

Without another thought, I ran straight at a nearby tree, used my foot to propel myself upwards, and grabbed the lowest branch I could. After that it was all a matter of simple muscle memory to pull myself from branch to branch, trying to ignore the persistent tingling in my legs.

"That's not the cabin," Hayden called, having seen my entire ascent into the foliage.

"I couldn't outrun it," I answered quite obviously.

The corpse came to a stop under the tree and turned its head skyward with a slow creaking movement. It didn't make any move to come after me, but it didn't leave either.

It simply stared at me with those dark holes where its eyes should have been.

It was bizarre that I was so out of breath and yet this monster didn't seem fazed at all by the run. He didn't take a single breath as he stared at me.

"I am ever so curious to see what the next part of your brilliant plan is," Hayden said with a smirk.

I ignored him. Figuring that if all he was going to do was make fun of me, I was better off without him. I had died after all. I was being chased by a psychotic zombie through some task I didn't understand. It wasn't like I was whining just to whine. I had a very legitimate reason to be upset at the moment.

The space between the tree and the door wasn't very far. If I hadn't been so high up, I might have been able to jump down from the tree and try to outrun the creature. But unfortunately, I was almost positive that if I jumped from this height, I'd break my ankles and be zombie dinner for sure.

Looking to the cabin, I realized that this wasn't as overly complicated as I was making it out to be. If I took the cannibalistic corpse out of the equation, I was just left with a puzzle that I needed to solve. The whole "fear of being eaten alive" thing was clouding my judgment and making me too scared to make an intelligent decision.

Why try to outrun the zombie to the cabin when I could just jump from a branch overhanging the roof?

It seemed so simple now that I realized what I should do that I almost laughed at myself for not having thought of it before.

"You seem happy," Hayden said, still sounding arrogant as usual.

I didn't give him the satisfaction of a response. Really, he'd probably just make fun of my idea and tell me I was going to get eaten for sure. So instead, I pulled my boots off to get a better grip with my bare feet and walked carefully along the tree branch until I was standing just over the roof of the building.

I'd jumped off enough swing sets as a kid to know that a hard landing could be an unpleasant thing on your legs, so with that knowledge, I braced myself as I jumped from the branch to the roof. The landing wasn't exactly graceful and I ended up rolling so far down that I almost fell off completely, but I managed to right myself in time to see the corpse running towards the cabin.

I can readily admit that split second decisions aren't my strong suit. There were two options sitting before me and I'd need to make my decision pretty quickly if I didn't want to be eaten. I could either sit there on the roof and let the zombie come after me, hoping he couldn't get up there, or I could jump right at that very second and try to get through the front door before it reached me.

"What are you waiting for?" Hayden yelled inside of the house, spurring me into action before I could really think about what I was doing.

With a loud yell I jumped off of the roof, boots in hand, and yanked on the front door as hard as I could; opening it with more force than I'd meant to. It took me all of two seconds to get inside and start shutting the door, though the corpse's arm that was now flailing wildly, was definitely blocking my path.

It felt like I was in a horror movie with the zombie's arm wedged in the door and me panting and yelling as I tried to shut it out. All I needed to do was lock the door, just like Hayden had said, and I'd be safe. I would have passed the first task.

Judging by how horrible the first task had been, I didn't even want to think about what the others would be like, or just how many I had in store for me.

"You can't just push his arm out for me? Is that *really* interfering that much?" I asked Hayden, still pushing against the wood of the door with all my might.

This zombie wasn't budging.

"Can't help you," he said again, lifting his hands up in surrender.

"I really don't like you," I panted, pushing hard enough that the creature finally withdrew its arm.

The door shut, I locked it, then I turned around and slid down the door into a pile of sweaty shock. There wasn't much more I could do. I was completely exhausted and really wanted to punch Hayden in the face as he smiled innocently at me, wrinkled his nose, and said, "Rough day, huh?"

CHAPTER 6

"What was that?" I asked, angrily getting to my feet and ignoring the pins-and-needles sensation that was now travelling through my entire body.

"I thought we decided to call it a zombie," Hayden retorted, throwing a few sticks of wood into the dusty fireplace and pulling a lighter out of his pants pocket.

"Not *that*," I spat, probably not making any sense at all. "Why did you leave me out there to die you--," I stopped myself, trying to keep from using a few choice swear words that had gotten my mouth washed out with soap as a kid.

Just because I was dead didn't mean I'd ignore all the good life lessons my mama had taught me.

"You almost did a good job out there," he answered,

finally managing to get a fire going. “Almost.”

“Oh, well I’m sorry I didn’t live up to your high standards of zombie dodging.”

“Maybe the next task will go a bit smoother,” he said with a shrug.

I really didn’t like this guy.

“What kind of place is this? What kind of afterlife makes you run away from zombies under the guise of completing an agility test?” I asked, sitting on an old wooden rocking chair and disturbing a few spiders that had been resting in the woodwork.

“Guise? Fancy word for someone so…,” he let his words trail off.

“What?” I asked threateningly, daring him to finish his sentence.

“Southern.”

“I graduated from a well-respected university yesterday, thank you very much,” I informed him.

“With a degree in vocal performance,” he pointed out. “Then you got yourself killed.”

“Oh yeah? Well what did you major in? How to piss people off?”

“Yeah, that was my major,” he deadpanned. “You know what your problem is?”

“I’m sure you’re going to tell me.”

“You worry about the wrong things. All of your anxiety is completely misplaced,” he said, his British accent getting thicker now that he was upset.

I wished I didn’t find the accent so alluring. Though I’d never admit that to Hayden. He didn’t need a reason for his ego to be inflated any more than it already was.

“How is it misplaced?” I asked, trying to keep my cool as he took a seat on the moldy bed across from me.

“You’re dead, Isla,” he said simply, as if that should explain his cryptic opinions. “You died last night and you haven’t said one word about being sad or upset. All you’ve done is worried about your family’s finances, or questioned my chivalry, or figure out some new and interesting way to make me want to throw you off a cliff.”

He shook his head in disbelief and threw me an eye roll.

“Aren’t you the least bit upset that your entire life was stolen away from you at such a young age?”

I didn’t say anything to him, not wanting to get into something so personal with someone so unfeeling. Of course I was upset, but as long as I didn’t explore those feelings, it would almost be like they weren’t real.

I may not have been scared of wolves or men, but I

was definitely terrified of my own weaknesses, and emotion was one of those weaknesses.

"What about the fact that you won't ever see your parents again? Does that bug you?"

"Are you trying to get a rise out of me or something? Because I don't really get what's going on here. Why do you care if I'm okay with being dead? Is that really part of your job description as my afterlife liaison?"

He shrugged his broad shoulders at me and laid down on the bed, placing his hands behind his head and closing his eyes.

"I don't care. I just think it's weird," he said.

It looked like he was done with the talking thing.

"You want to talk about weird things? Why can't you tell me what you did before you became a Guide?" I asked, fully aware that my voice was squeakier than normal because of my heightened emotional state. "You must know how you got here. So why can't you tell me any personal information?"

"What if I told you it was against the rules to give you any information about my own personal life?"

"Would you be lying?"

"Yes, but would it shut you up?" he asked, mimicking my voice once more.

"You're rude," I told him. "Needlessly rude; which is the worst kind of rude to be."

"There's a good kind of rude?"

"Why are you still here? Now that I've finished the first task can't you leave me alone for a while?" I asked, wanting nothing more than to be alone right at that moment.

In all honestly, having company would have been nice to keep me from thinking too much about the questions Hayden had asked me. I didn't want to think about how much I'd miss my family or how unfair it was that my entire life was now gone. But Hayden wasn't good company and so I thought having to deal with those unpleasant demons would be better than sitting in a room with him for another second.

"I have to stay until the end of the cycle," he responded, as if that response should have made perfect sense to me when all it did was confuse me more.

"Cycle?"

"Each day is a cycle. You get one task per cycle and I have to stay with you through the entire thing."

"So when is the cycle over so you can leave?" I asked, being sarcastically sweet to him.

"Trust me love, I want to leave just as badly as you

want me out of here. Don't you think I have better things to do than sit around all day listening to you drone on with that awful, slow accent?"

"Do you?" I asked.

"Obviously."

"When is it over?" I asked again, since he had opted for a snarky comment the first time I'd asked him that same question. Maybe if I kept asking, one day he'd finally answer me.

"Once the snow starts to fall, I can leave," he said cryptically.

I glanced out the window at the foggy woods. It had been chilly once the sun had disappeared but I wouldn't say it was snow weather. It just wasn't cold enough.

"Please don't state the obvious and tell me it's not cold enough for snow," he said, stopping me before I could voice that exact thought.

"Well it's not," I mumbled in response.

"It's also impossible for zombies to be real," he pointed out, reminding me (not so subtly) that I was dead and the rules of life had changed.

"What was with the zombie thing anyway? I didn't really picture the path to heaven littered with zombies."

"Zombies scare you, so that's what came to motivate

you," he responded.

"Zombies don't scare me," I protested with a nervous laugh.

"Listen. I don't make this stuff up. I didn't come up with the creepy running corpse thing. That came out of your own imagination. You have way more control over this world than you think you do," he said. "Besides, you snuck out of bed when you were nine and watched a zombie movie your parents had rented and you've been terrified of them ever since."

My mouth hung open in shock that someone I had just met could know a detail about me that was so intimate. I hadn't even told Tuck and Monica about that night. Mostly because I was embarrassed that, out of all the things in the world I could be scared of, zombies was at the top of my list.

Still, it could have easily been a lucky guess.

"Who told you that?" I asked.

"No one had to tell me. I'm your Guide, remember? I know things."

"Yeah, but things about my nine-year-old self? Why would that even be useful?"

Hayden didn't respond. Instead he just gestured to the dark, dirty cabin we were currently stuck in as if the answer to that question should be painfully obvious.

I guess it was a stupid question.

"How many people have you guided?" I asked, wanting to change the subject.

"Just one other girl," he said, his eyes trained on the ceiling very pointedly as he lay on his back.

"Were you this mean to her?"

"The job does bring out some of my less desirable traits I guess," he began, making the biggest understatement ever spoken. "But she was my cousin so I was definitely nicer to her."

"Cousin?" I asked, my interest suddenly piqued. "So you did have a life before this."

"It's not important," he said, sounding like we were treading on dangerous ground.

"Did she make it to her Destination?"

Hayden was quiet for a long time. I couldn't tell if he was hesitant to answer me or if he was just completely ignoring me like he usually did.

"No," he finally said after a long silence. "She didn't."

I mulled this over for a moment.

It was possible to fail this series of tests, which made them infinitely scarier. But the scariest thing was not knowing what that actually meant.

"What happens if we don't make it to our Destination?"

"I don't remember," Hayden said.

"How can you not remember something like that?" I asked incredulously.

I realized I should have been a little nicer to him since he was opening up about his cousin and he hadn't made a snarky comment in the last few minutes, but it just didn't make sense to me that he could forget such a monumental detail.

"Things get a bit cloudy when I get here at the beginning of a cycle," he said gruffly, indicating to me that our time of "open discussion" was quickly coming to a close.

"Does that mean you can't remember what you did before this? You must remember something if you can recall your cousin," I pointed out gently, trying to sound as unobtrusive as possible.

"We're done talking about this," he said with a note of finality.

Honestly, I was surprised I'd gotten that much out of him. He didn't really seem like the type to share his feelings with the class.

Still, he wasn't all snark and threats and that gave me a

small glimmer of hope that he wasn't completely soulless.

We sat in silence for a while, me trying not to think about my family or my stolen life and Hayden brooding and giving me the silent treatment. It was a good forty minutes or so when the snow finally started to fall. Only it wasn't just falling outside. Delicate white flakes made their way through nonexistent cracks in the ceiling, landing on my bare shoulders and making me shiver.

"It's cold," I commented, quite obviously.

"It's snow," Hayden pointed out in exasperation.

"So does this mean you're leaving?" I asked, yawning loudly and finding that I suddenly had an overwhelming urge to kick him off of the dusty bed and take it for myself.

"Sadly, our riveting conversation will be over in about thirty seconds when you fall asleep."

"Sorry," I said, more out of habit than anything else. "I'm not sure why I'm so tired all of a sudden."

"It's the snow," Hayden said, making absolutely no sense at all.

Maybe it was my exhaustion setting in and he had actually said something that was completely logical. My tired mind had just botched it all up.

Wordlessly, he stood from the bed and ushered me over to it, almost seeming kind. Almost.

“I guess I’ll deal with you tomorrow. Try not to make a mess of things too much while I’m gone,” he said.

I opened my mouth to throw some witty insult back at him but found that my entire body felt as if it were shutting down involuntarily. It was the same sensation I got when a doctor put me under and I tried as hard as I could to stay awake. It was a losing battle to say the least.

My eyes became fuzzy and my lids heavy as I tried to ask Hayden one last question that never came out. I had to know if I’d be safe in the cabin after he left. Instead, I gave in to the overwhelming urge to let sleep take me as I watched my Guide disappear through the front door, leaving it unlocked behind him.

CHAPTER 7

I woke the next morning feeling sore, achy, and warm. The "sore and achy" I'd expected. I wasn't out of shape because of Monica's mandatory apartment-weekly-yoga she'd instated, but I didn't work out every day, so running for my life from a zombie hadn't really been something I'd trained for.

I could feel the sun beating down on my closed lids, which surprised me to no end, since the last time I'd been awake it was foggy and snowy. Apparently weather was very unpredictable in purgatory. I'd have to make a note of that somewhere in my "What I Did on my Purgatory Vacation" essay I presented to the class. This nonexistent essay would probably consist of three things: unpredictable weather, stupid challenges that seemed completely irrelevant, and rude but highly attractive British men.

Really, if Hayden wasn't so completely unpleasant, my stay in purgatory wouldn't be all that bad. But no. Mr. Bad Boy had to have an attitude.

Opening my eyes wearily, I glanced around the room, surprised that I'd been so anxious to hop into the completely disgusting bed I was currently lying on. The sheets were dusty, the mattress reeked of mold, and the entire bedframe was covered in spider webs. The only explanation I could come up with for my desire to sleep somewhere so horrible, was the fact that the snow made me sleep… somehow… because that made all the sense in the world.

Logic told me that I probably needed to eat something for breakfast, but as I stood and walked around the dusty cabin room, I didn't feel hungry at all. It was probably just as well since it didn't look like the room contained any food that hadn't expired over 100 years ago anyway.

I heaved a heavy sigh, very pointedly ignoring the homesick feeling that was beginning to spread at the thought of my family and what they might be doing today.

Would they be picking out a coffin? Or was it too soon for that? How long did people generally wait until they buried someone anyway?

I shivered at the thought that my body might be lying in a morgue somewhere surrounded by other dead bodies. Everything sterile, cold, and metal. Absolutely no warmth or life. And to top it all off I absolutely hated the smell of formaldehyde, which would undoubtedly be a permanent fixture in the morgue.

Those were the thoughts I needed to keep at bay. Maybe when all of these tasks were done, I'd let myself think about my family, or all of the things I'd wanted to do before I died. But for now, I was going to focus on the task at hand and just try to survive through the cycles and Hayden's attitude. Though I wasn't sure which was worse.

"I hope Monica remembered to feed Ron Swanson," I thought aloud, my nonexistent hunger reminding me that Monica might forget her responsibilities in light of her roommate/best friend dying.

Our Scottish Fold looked grumpy enough when he had enough to eat. I couldn't imagine what his smushed up little face would look like if he wasn't being fed.

Killing time until my unwilling Guide showed up, I examined the cabin more closely, feeling like it looked more like a haunted house than anything. My cousin Brighton would have loved it. She liked to pretend she was a ghost hunter. And she was yet another person I'd never seen again.

I wasn't too keen to get outside just in case the zombie from yesterday decided to stick around. Of course I could always look out the windows, but the shutters seemed to be stuck, only letting in the tiny beam of light I had woken to that snuck between the wooden planks.

Sitting down on the moldy bed again, I felt myself shiver involuntarily as I replayed the traumatic scene from yesterday. The cabin was quiet; the sound muffled by the layers of dust that coated every surface. But somewhere, I could vaguely hear what sounded like crying.

Not just crying, but a woman crying.

"Mama?" I whispered to the empty room, wondering if my mind was playing tricks on me.

"My little girl," she whispered back, her voice broken and difficult to hear.

Was I actually hearing my mother? Was my spirit somehow still linked to my body?

"Mama?" I said again, this time a bit louder, hoping that by some miracle she could hear me.

I looked around the room, desperate to find some indication that she could hear what I was saying.

Though the sound was still muffled, I could have sworn my brother's voice came next, saying, "I can't believe this happened."

"Tuck!" I shouted, overjoyed to hear his voice, but instantly saddened by the reminder that I could no longer see him.

Forgetting about my fears, I opened the door to the cabin and ran out into the thick fog. Apparently the beautiful sunny day had disappeared the second I stepped outside. I could barely see my hand in front of my face but I could tell right away that the ground felt different than it had the day before.

Where dirt and plants had padded the ground before, there was now thick, lush grass. It was almost as if the cabin weren't in the same place as it was yesterday. Of course that didn't make any sense. But none of my experience in this place had made sense so far.

"Tuck?" I called again, now running blindly through the fog that had so quickly replaced the sunlight, not concerned with the cabin that I could no longer see. "I can hear you, Tuck."

"Are you completely insane? Get back here!" Hayden yelled, pulling me back forcefully by the arm so that I spun around and hit his chest painfully.

"That hurt," I shouted at him, mostly angry that he had scared me so badly and less concerned with the iron tight grip he had on my upper arm at the moment.

"Not as much as falling off the island, genius," he retorted coolly, nodding over my shoulder into the fog. "I don't need you failing the second task before it even starts."

I looked behind me, trying to understand what he was talking about. I still wasn't sure when the sun had disappeared and left me with the impenetrable curtain of fog, but it made it very difficult to make out my surroundings.

"Let me help you," he said.

Hayden pulled on my arm, yanking me down to the ground with him so that we were on our hands and knees. He looked over at me with an annoyed raise of his eyebrow, his face only inches from mine.

"Look down there," he said, nodding to the grass in front of us and finally releasing my arm, leaving a bright red mark where his hand had been only moments before.

Something told me he wasn't too concerned with hurting me since I plagued his existence with pleasant conversation.

Trying to ignore the fact that Hayden had so unexpectedly doomed my day with his angst, I crawled forward a bit, letting my hands feel the ground in front of me to avoid whatever hazard he was trying to show me. It only took a few seconds to see why he had been so forceful with me (besides the obvious reason that it gave him a good excuse to manhandle me and inflict at least a little pain). The grass ended suddenly and dropped off into nothingness.

I would have called it a cliff if I could see the bottom of the drop off, or even if I could see the earth below the grass. But from what I could observe, the grassy hill I was perched on didn't drop off into a cliff. It simply ended. As if the entire hill were floating in midair.

"This hill--."

"Island," Hayden corrected.

"Island," I said, trying the word on for size but not quite liking the description for our current environment. "It's… what? Floating?"

"Like I said Casper, I don't make up the rules. This place is all you."

"But when would I ever imagine up a floating island? It doesn't make any sense," I asked, standing with him and backing away from the edge carefully.

"Your brother Tucker was playing a video game when you guys were in high school and you saw it there," Hayden told me, reporting back details of my life in such a matter-of-fact way that I almost believed it wasn't weird.

"How did you--."

"I already told you. I'm your Guide. I know things."

"Except what you did before you got here," I said.

I knew it was a low blow but I was so sick of his smug grin that I had to do something to put him in his place.

"We're going to be late for your second task," he answered simply.

It was obvious that he liked me even less than I liked him and simply wanted to get the tasks over with as soon as possible so that he could get rid of me.

Of course I didn't understand why he didn't just let me fall off the edge of the island. That would have saved him a lot of trouble in the long run. Then again, if his job was to get me to my Destination, I guess he had to follow those rules no matter how little he cared for me. He had to do his job the best he could.

"Shouldn't we be walking a little slower so we don't fall off this island and die?" I asked Hayden in a sing song voice.

The fog was so thick that I knew by the time we saw a drop off it would be too late. We would have just walked casually to our deaths… our second deaths I guess.

"If you hadn't taken a little detour this morning, we

wouldn't have to walk so fast now," he answered.

"I thought I heard something."

"Great, now you've gone nuts. Normally we wait until the last task for that bit to kick in, but it's good that you're getting an early start on it," he said dryly.

The dewy grass squeaked under our feet and I suddenly wished I could take off my cowboy boots and just enjoy the less-than-sunny day, rather than following a grumpy British guy to a task that would probably force me to do all sorts of unpleasant things.

"Who did you hear?" he asked after a few minutes of us walking in silence.

To say that I was surprised to hear Hayden ask me a personal question was the understatement of the century. I wasn't sure what his angle was, but I knew he couldn't just be asking to be nice. It wasn't like him.

"I thought I heard my mom," I told him timidly. I didn't want to sound too crazy. "And then my brother."

Hayden didn't say anything to my remarks; he simply kept up his impossible pace that required me to do an awkward half jog by his side.

"Well?" I said in annoyance.

"Well, what?"

"Well, what does that mean?"

“That you’re crazy? I don’t know,” he said, sounding much more like his old self again.

“Ugh. What is that, your new catch phrase?” I asked. “’I don’t know.’ ‘I don’t know’,” I said in the best imitation of his voice that I could muster.

It was a pretty awful imitation. My British accent wasn’t exactly up to scratch.

He didn’t respond (surprise, surprise) but instead kept walking in silence.

The fog was slowly lessening and I could just make out the hazy surroundings that were veiled in mystery only moments before. From what I could tell (and I couldn’t tell much), it looked like we were surrounded by a number of floating islands just like the one we were currently standing on.

Each one kind of resembled an ice cream cone of earth with a grassy hill on top; a few trees and small rivers dotting the surface. Thick tree roots stuck out of the ground all around the sides of the earth, and each island spun in slow, lazy rotations.

“Please don’t tell me I’m going to be chased again today,” I said, whining a bit but not really caring at the moment.

It wasn’t like I could make Hayden think less of me at

that point. It was a mathematical impossibility.

"Second task: Motor Skills," he answered, just as vague as ever.

I gave him a skeptical look, knowing that the task was sure to be overkill just to test out such a simple ability.

"Can't I just complete the sobriety test or something?" I asked.

"Familiar with that test, are we?" he asked back, shutting me up.

We walked in silence. Again. As usual. Until we came to the opposite end of the island where Hayden abruptly stopped and looked over at me expectantly.

"What?"

"Get on with the test," he responded, sounding like I definitely shouldn't have to ask him what he was talking about.

"What do you want me to do? Touch my finger to my nose or something?"

"No, I want you to jump.".

CHAPTER 8

"I'm sorry, what?" I asked Hayden, sure that I had misheard what he'd said.

"I want you to jump," he repeated in the calmest voice I'd ever heard.

"Weren't you the person who just called me all sorts of horrible things for almost walking off the edge of the island?" I asked. I needed to clarify that he was, in fact, just as crazy as he was coming off at the moment.

"That was on *that* side of the island," he said with a smirk. "Now that we're on *this* side, I want you to jump."

"Oh, is that all?" I asked sarcastically. "And why, exactly, am I doing this?"

"Motor skills," he said, like I was an idiot.

"What does jumping off of a cliff have to do with

motor skills?"

"See that island in the distance?" he asked me, pointing straight ahead at a large, rotating island a good fifteen or twenty feet away.

"I definitely can't jump to that," I informed him.

Though really, that shouldn't be the type of thing you needed to point out to someone. I'd hope that information was pretty obvious.

"No, not that one," he said in annoyance. "The one beyond that."

I squinted my eyes in the fog, trying to see what he was talking about but failing miserably. I could see a faint purple light in the distance, somewhere even higher up than the island we were standing on at the moment.

"The light?" I asked finally.

"That light is actually a stone set in a tree trunk on another island," he said.

It almost sounded as if he had given this information hundreds of times and was now reciting it because he had to. Of course I knew that wasn't the case because A) he'd only ever guided one other person and B) he'd said that I invented this entire place so he couldn't have seen it before.

"And I have to get to the light?"

"The light is where the safe house is," he confirmed

with a somber nod.

I assessed the light in the distance, now understanding what I had to do. Somehow, Hayden wanted me to get from island to island until I reached the safe house. Of course I didn't really think this exercise had anything to do with motor skills, but I also didn't think pointing that out to him would do any good. At best he'd probably just brood some more.

"Will something be chasing me this time?" I asked, wondering if I could at least catch a break on the whole zombie thing today.

"I think this task is difficult enough without any motivation for you. Besides, it's not about speed today; it's about your hand-eye coordination."

"And upper body strength," I added, not sure I could really pull myself up onto the island from the dangling roots I'd undoubtedly have to grab when I failed to jump to the grass.

"And that," he agreed.

"Should I just get to it then?" I asked hesitantly.

"Would it make you feel better if I shouted 'go' or counted you off or something?"

I didn't dignify his snarky question with a response. I simply looked up at him through my eyelashes, trying to convey just how annoyed I was with him right at that moment.

“One, two, three,” he deadpanned.

“Thank you for that,” I said, walking to the very edge of the island and trying to gauge the gap between the two land masses.

Of course both islands kept rotating slowly, meaning that if I wanted to stay lined up with the other one I had to keep walking to the right. That little detail was actually much more annoying than I would have thought when compared to the task that lay before me.

“I’m just going to run and jump and hope for the best,” I told him, trying to give myself a little pep talk.

“I’ll be waiting,” he answered.

“Okay. Here I go,” I said, taking a deep breath and a few steps back.

I ran as fast as I could, my eyes trained on a tree root sticking out of the light brown earth a few feet under the opposite island. Of course the second I got to the edge of the grass I stopped dead in my tracks and took a few steps away from the precarious edge.

“Very impressive,” Hayden said sarcastically, giving me an arrogant slow clap. The guy could be such a tool. “Please do that a few more times just to make sure we’ve thoroughly exhausted the possibility that the island is going to come to you."

"You try it if it's so easy," I said in annoyance.

I gave myself a mental and physical shake, trying to get rid of the screaming voice in my brain telling me it was completely insane to jump from one impossible floating island to another, hoping I could grab a tree root on the way down, then somehow manage to pull myself up mountain-climber style, without any kind of harness. I definitely wasn't under the illusion that I was some sort of action hero. On my best day I could get halfway up the rock wall at the mini golf place. And now, somehow, I had to complete this task that no sane person would ever attempt?

"Am I being punished for something?" I asked Hayden.

"Excuse me?"

"Punished," I said again, slowly this time so that he couldn't misunderstand me. "Is this because I took my dad's car that night in high school before I had my license? Because I definitely had my driver's permit so it wasn't as bad as it sounded."

"What are you going on about now?" Hayden seemed genuinely confused by my sudden barrage of questions.

"Or maybe it's because I kissed Bobby Pikitis at that

school dance in junior high when I was supposed to be telling him my friend sort of liked him," I went on, now trying to remember every bad thing I'd ever done. "I did cheat that one time Tuck and I were playing poker to see who would have to pull the weeds in the backyard."

"Please, stop talking," Hayden said with a sigh.

He had started rubbing his temples with his eyes closed, apparently trying to keep his cool.

"Oh no," I gasped.

"What?"

"It's because I lied to Mama about who really dropped her box full of china from Grandma," I confessed with a hand over my mouth, my eyes wide. "I said my cousin Reagan knocked it off the shelf in the garage when she came to North Carolina to visit."

"I beg of you. Stop talking."

"She got into so much trouble," I told him, shaking my head guiltily. "Her mom didn't let her play her favorite video game for a month. I'd almost forgotten about that."

"Just shut up and get to the island!" Hayden finally yelled, apparently no longer able to contain his rage that already bubbled so close to the surface.

"You don't have to be so bossy about it," I said huffily. "All right, take two."

Following the same pattern as before, I gave myself a running start, kept a determined gaze on my goal, and stopped right before I got to the edge.

"I can't do it," I wailed. "The island is too far! And if I don't grab any of those roots on the way down I'll fall to my death."

"You're already dead," he pointed out, quite unnecessarily.

"Fine, I'll die again. I'll fail to reach my Destination and you'll have a track record of oh for two."

"The island isn't as far as it looks, just run, jump, and grab any tree root you see," he told me.

Of course he had to make it sound like the easiest thing in the world.

"Fine," I said simply, going back to my starting position once more, running, and failing to jump again.

"You have got to be kidding me," Hayden said in exasperation. "I can't take much more of this. My ten-year-old cousin had harder tasks than this and completed them in half the time."

Except that she didn't make it to the end, I thought, knowing that this fact was too sensitive to actually bring up. Still, I couldn't ignore the fact that it was possible for me to fail and, looking at the impossible floating island, the odds were not in my favor.

"Would it make you feel better if I did it with you?" Hayden asked, his brow furrowed in a concerned manner.

It had to be a trick.

"I thought you couldn't help me," I asked suspiciously.

"It wouldn't be helping you physically. It would just be offering some moral support if I made the jump with you," he answered reasonably.

I looked him over for a moment, wondering why he had suddenly turned nice and still sure it couldn't be genuine.

"Isla," he said, placing his hands on my bare shoulders and looking at me with his icy blue eyes. "I want to make the jump with you, okay?"

He was so close to me that I could smell his cologne and suddenly I felt as if I couldn't breathe properly. How could I go from hating him to being flustered by him so quickly? Sure he was sort of gorgeous and had that whole "bad boy with an accent" thing going for him, but he also happened to be the rudest person I'd ever met and completely unhelpful when I was facing death or death again circumstances.

Except for this moment.

For some unknown reason, Hayden had decided to

grow a conscious right at the moment I needed his help desperately.

"We can do this," he whispered to me, his thumb tracing little circles on my bare shoulder.

I hated myself for noticing how close his face was to mine and tried to regain some sense of composure.

"Okay," I said with a dopey smile.

So much for my dignity.

Hayden took my hand and walked with me back to my starting point.

"Just let me know when you're ready," he said supportively, giving my hand a little squeeze.

"Okay?" I said, sounding very confused over this personality change. "I think I'm ready."

"Great. Here we go."

With that, we both began to run full speed, Hayden holding on to my hand so tightly that I couldn't back out of the jump even if I wanted to. If I suddenly stopped running, I'd mess up Hayden's speed. I might not go over the edge but he definitely would and it would be all my fault.

There was no other option. I had to do it.

Screaming as loud as I could right before I got to the ledge, Hayden suddenly released my hand, slowed his pace, and gave me one extremely violent push right in the middle of my back. My feet left the ground and the air left my lungs from the force of his hands on my back, and before I knew it, I was sailing through the air, arms flailing ungracefully all around me and my mind going crazy with a million thoughts at once.

I was angry at Hayden for tricking me, panicked at the fact that there was an endless amount of open air below my feet, and determined to grab at least one of the tree roots sticking out of the earth in front of me without being impaled by them.

There wasn't much room for error in the split second that I had to grab onto whatever came into my grasp. If I didn't manage to stop my fall, I'd definitely be a goner, and something told me the unknown for those who didn't reach their Destination was not a pleasant place.

Letting out one final scream, I threw my hands out in front of me, unable to see from all the wavy white-blonde hair that flew in front of my face.

With a horrible thud and a white hot pain in my middle finger, I grabbed onto the damp tree roots that miraculously held my weight. I pressed my cheek against the wet earth and clung for dear death to the side of the island, not looking up or down, simply panting and hating Hayden.

"Start climbing," his very unwelcome voice said

directly above me.

How on earth had he gotten onto the island?

“I hate you!” I screamed, my entire body shaking from just how terrified I was at that moment.

The endless expanse of air below me was scary, but knowing that I didn’t have the arm strength to pull myself onto the island and get out of this alive was the scariest part. At what point did I finally admit to myself that I couldn’t do it and just let go?

“I don’t care for you much either. Now stop being completely useless and start climbing.”

I hadn’t ever been a rage filled person. In fact, before I’d died I couldn’t name a single person I hated. Sure there were some girls I didn’t like much and a few cheating ex-boyfriends I’d rather not see. But no one I hated.

At that moment, clinging to the dirty tree root like it was my only hope, I could very truthfully say, I hated Hayden.

With a deep burning passion.

“I can’t do it,” I called up to him, setting aside my hate in favor of my logic that told me I somehow needed to climb.

“Yeah, I know,” he said, not encouraging me at all. “If you can’t even do this, there’s no way you’ll pass the other tasks. You might as well just give up now."

"Aren't you supposed to be rooting for me?" I asked incredulously. "Don't you need me to make it to my Destination so you can get a raise or something?"

"After listening to all your whining, I'm not sure it's worth it," he told me, shrugging his shoulders and walking away from the ledge.

He couldn't be serious. There was no way he wanted me to drop off a cliff just because I had whined a little (rightfully so might I add) about being dead.

Slowly and carefully, I released the tree root with one hand and stretched it skyward towards the next root, closing my sore fingers around it and finding that I was still completely stuck. I couldn't look down to see where I should put my foot. I couldn't just hoist myself up and hope the root held me.

Unless I was willing to suddenly become daring, there wasn't really much I could do but stay there like a squirrel stuck halfway up a tree trunk. In this scenario, I saw Hayden as the mean little kid with a BB gun, repeatedly trying to fire at me.

I definitely couldn't die here (again) so I took a deep breath, steadied my nerves, and pulled myself up to the next tree root. My feet scrambled for purchase for a minute but eventually found it, however unsteadily. The boots hadn't been a great choice for my little mountain climbing experience. They had no tread, and were completely stiff and inflexible. I couldn't have picked worse footwear if I'd tried.

It was a slow long process to get myself up to the edge of the island. I was sweaty and terrified by the time the grass was within my reach and my entire body shook with the constant effort of keeping myself from falling. I wasn't sure exactly how long it had taken me, but it felt like hours had passed in silence as I maintained a slow and steady panic.

"About time," Hayden said, peeking his head over the side of the grass and looking completely bored.

"Hayden, I need you to give me your hand. There are no more roots and I can't grab the grass without pulling it all out," I told him evenly.

I knew he was a complete jerk but could it really be that difficult for him to just reach out his hand and help me up? I'd made the entire climb myself and now needed one small favor from him that would barely expend an ounce of his energy.

"No can do, kiddo," he said simply, getting down so that he was lying on his stomach with his chin resting on his hands.

"Seriously? I need one thing. You can't just do this for me?" I asked, now getting mad.

"I told you, I can't help you."

"You pushed me off the other island. Wasn't that helping me?"

"That was purely recreational. If I didn't push you off the edge in a productive way, I probably would have done it later on down the line just for sport," he informed me.

"Hayden, please," I pleaded. "I'm so tired. I don' think I can pull myself up. I've done so much, just please help me with this one thing."

I didn't really want to beg, especially when it came to him. But I also didn't want to die again and go wherever the task failures went. If this was what purgatory was like, I could only imagine what the other place would hold in store for those who failed.

As I clung shakily to the ledge, I couldn't help but think that it was odd that we'd walked so far yesterday and I hadn't even broken a sweat, but now I was exhausted; though walking a long distance and suddenly becoming a pro mountain climber were definitely two different things.

Hayden shrugged his shoulders at me once more from his position on the grass and I tried my hardest not to cry. I wasn't sad by any means, but I could feel the tears of rage building inside of me and those were the worst kind. That was what preceded an ugly cry.

Burying my emotions deep within me, I reached my small hand up as far as I could and closed my fingers around a fistful of grass that I was sure would rip from the earth the second I put any weight on it. I brought one foot up to a higher root, trying to find purchase on the wet earth and hoping that I wouldn't accidentally propel myself backwards off the edge of the island right when I'd almost made it to the top.

"You do realize you've doubled the time we normally spend in a cycle and you aren't even close to the end of this task yet, right?" Hayden asked, now rolling over onto his back and placing his hands behind his head lazily. "You still have to do this all over again on the next island."

He wasn't very good at encouraging people. He could definitely check motivational speaker off the list of things he might have done before becoming a Guide.

I didn't really have enough strength to yell at him and climb at the same time so I opted for the one that kept me alive… sort of.

Taking one last deep breath, I hoisted myself up onto the top of the island. The handful of grass pulled away from the earth a bit but held firm enough for me to complete the action, and the second I touched the top soil I fell onto my back next to Hayden, breathing heavily and having no idea how I could possibly do that a second time.

"Ready for the next one?" he asked me, tilting his head so that he was facing me, his nose almost touching my cheek.

"I want to hit you so badly right now, but I'm too tired," I said, furrowing my brow and ignoring the sweat I could feel beading there.

"Stop being such a baby. Besides, the next one isn't nearly as bad," he said, sitting up and walking away from me.

Apparently he expected me to follow behind without taking a few moments to rest first. I knew that arguing with him was futile, and even if I did try to point out the fact that I'd just completed a very difficult task, he'd just say I was being weak, or something equally as obnoxious.

"Oh and by the way, you got your dress dirty," he called as he continued to move away from me.

Looking down at my mud streaked white lace dress, I could see that he was right, though it seemed like a cruel thing to point out when he knew full well I couldn't do anything about it.

I stood from the grass and turned to take one last look at the sheer cliff I had just scaled, then looked back at Hayden's retreating form. Maybe falling from the island wouldn't have been such a bad thing.

CHAPTER 9

I could feel the damp grass slowly soaking the bottom of my dress as I sat with my bare feet dangling over the edge of the island. I knew I'd have a very unattractive wet spot right on my bum the second I stood up, but I wasn't planning on standing any time soon so it didn't really matter. At the moment I was too preoccupied with tilting my head up towards the non-existent sun in the foggy sky, my eyes closed and a small smile on my lips.

Maybe I'd get one of those overcast tans you get at the beach, that way I wouldn't look like such a ghost with my pale skin.

"What do you mean, 'no'?" Hayden asked me, working himself up into a rage as he paced back and forth on the grass.

He had some serious anger management issues.

"This task is ridiculous, Hayden," I responded, almost laughing as I said it. "What in the world does climbing a floating cliff have to do with motor skills? It doesn't make any sense and I refuse to participate in the madness any longer."

"So, what? You're just going to sit here and rot away?"

"This place is beautiful," I answered.

"Get up," he said quietly, his voice actually quite threatening.

"No," I replied primly. "I like it here and I don't have the energy to climb another cliff. If that makes you mad then you can leave. You haven't been the most pleasant company to have around anyway."

It was true that Hayden was sort of trying to help me, but he'd been so rude since the first second we'd met that I really wouldn't have minded getting rid of him at that point. My afterlife would have been a much more pleasant place without him in it and I couldn't deny that after my last terrifying climb, I could use some alone time to just relax.

Hayden didn't say anything, but instead hooked me under each arm and pulled me to my feet, almost accidentally knocking me over the edge of the cliff in the process.

"Go," he commanded, pointing to the adjacent island like I was a dog he was scolding.

"You're not the boss of me," I said like a five-year-old, sticking my chin out defiantly.

I wasn't a weak girl. I didn't have to take crap from this guy no matter who he was. Daddy would have had a fit if he'd heard half of the things Hayden had said to me.

"Isla, so help me, if you don't jump to that other island, I'm going to push you over the ledge," he said, bringing his face close to mine and letting his eyes bore into my soul.

"Oh no! Hayden's going to push me over the edge," I mocked, bringing my hands up over my mouth and making my eyes wide.

I wasn't quite sure where I'd gotten all that courage, especially when I didn't doubt for a second that he'd follow through on his threat. Maybe it was because the idea of falling to my second death was actually more desirable than having to climb up another cliff side that would probably have the same result.

"If you're not going to complete the tasks then you're of no use to me. And if you're of no use to me there's no reason for me to keep you around, wasting my time," he whispered, his face still close to mine.

“Is that speech how you woo all the ladies?” I asked, quickly giving him a kiss on the cheek, then laughing at how hard he was working to maintain the bad boy image on my behalf.

Without warning, I felt his hands on my side in a motion that knocked the wind out of me, then I felt nothing but my stomach dropping as I went over the edge. I didn’t make a sound in that second of free fall before Hayden’s hand closed around my wrist, catching me just before I fell out of his reach. I swung like a pendulum into the side of the island, hitting it painfully.

“What is wrong with you?” I asked breathlessly, still dangling by the one limp arm Hayden held.

“I warned you already but you didn’t believe me. Now are you going to complete the task or not?” he asked. “I can’t hold on to you forever.”

“I’ll do it!” I yelled, terrified that he might actually drop me.

“That’s more like it.”

Almost effortlessly, Hayden pulled me back onto the grass and released me.

“Now get to it,” he said, nodding to the island that held another step to my Destination.

I didn't speak, now actually quite scared of Hayden and his completely unstable moods. When he was pretending to be all dark and brooding he wasn't all that scary, but what kind of psychopath dangled a girl over a ledge just to get her to cooperate?

He clearly had some unresolved childhood issues that he liked to take out on women. Maybe he had been some creepy serial killer in his past life. Or maybe he'd been a young Norman Bates type. That would explain why he was now sentenced to a life guiding the lost. Perhaps it was supposed to be ironic punishment.

Giving myself enough space for a running start, I stared at the adjacent island. Luckily, this cliff side wasn't as sheer as the last one. Small ledges and overhangs jutted out of the earth every few feet, making me believe that if I could just jump far enough, my climb up to the grass wouldn't be all that difficult.

My legs were shaking and I knew normally I'd have to do my "run and stop at the last second" routine a few times. But the way Hayden had looked at me as I was swinging over the ledge, my life completely in his hands, made me feel like the risk of falling was better than staying here with him for one more second. Besides, if I stopped before jumping he'd probably count that as the final straw and toss me overboard.

Taking one last deep breath, I ran as fast as I could and propelled myself forward off the relative safety of the grass. I flew through the air for one breathtaking moment, letting the breeze buoy me up a bit, before landing hard on one of the outcropping ledges. It had escaped my notice until that moment that I'd left my boots on the other island but I'd just have to do without them. There was absolutely no way to go back and I knew Hayden would already be waiting for me at the safe house.

Climbing from ledge to ledge and refusing to look back at the fall I'd have to face if I slipped, I considered my options.

Once I reached the top of the cliff side I'd be forced to spend time in the safe house with Hayden and his multiple personalities. I couldn't refuse to join him or refuse to do the tasks because I was pretty sure he'd murder me if I did.

Like I'd said, I wasn't a weak girl, but I also wasn't a stupid girl and I'd seen enough of my friends date guys with short tempers to know that Hayden was more dangerous than I'd originally thought. He really might have been a full blown crazy person.

Coming to the last ledge and feeling completely shocked that I'd already made the climb, I carefully stood on the grassy island top, looking around for any sign of my unstable Guide.

The tree with the glowing purple stone in the trunk could be seen in the distance and despite the thick fog, I could easily pick my way through the field to my destination. The trunk had a sizeable split right under the stone and the stairs carved into the dirt floor were a pretty safe indication that I'd come to the right spot.

The cool earth stairs felt good on my bare feet, and I let one pale finger trace the wall as I walked deeper into the ground. The stairs ended abruptly at a wooden door with a warm orange light shining through the open gap at the bottom of the wood. Though I knew Hayden would undoubtedly be inside, unhappy that I'd survived the task, I had to go in if I wanted any hope of reaching my final Destination.

I lifted my chin into the air as I entered the room, ready for a fight. The room was pretty small, and closely resembled the cabin we'd stayed in the night before, though this room very obviously lacked any windows. The floor was dirt as were the walls and the ceiling, but a warm fire popped and hissed in the fireplace and the bed was open so I walked over and took a seat across from Hayden.

He rocked gently back and forth in the old wooden

rocking chair and kept his gaze trained on the fire. I was sure he was probably trying to suppress his rage or think of the best way to kill me in a fireplace, so I didn't interrupt his thoughts.

I'd had a dark nagging feeling in the pit of my stomach all day but I'd avoided examining it, knowing I'd need my full concentration to face the ill named motor skills task. Now, as Hayden and I sat in awkward silence, I pulled the issue from the recesses of my memory to examine the troubling fact in the light of a calm room.

Hayden had only ever guided one other person before. That person was his cousin. And that person hadn't ever reached their Destination.

It was no surprise that Hayden wasn't the most emotional guy in the world. He was mean and gruff and really unpleasant. But I also didn't doubt that he loved his cousin and really wanted her to make it to her Destination.

And then there was me.

The girl who bugged him to no end.

He couldn't stand me and suddenly I was placing my life and my trust in his hands. If Hayden hadn't even been able to get his cousin to her Destination, then I was positive I had absolutely no hope. I was more likely to get killed off because Hayden purposefully messed me up just to get rid of me. The tasks were difficult enough as it was, I didn't need the one person who was supposed to be offering their help, out to get me.

My choice was clear.

Somehow I had to get away from Hayden and find a way to complete the tasks on my own. Either that or I had to watch my back every second I was around him to make sure he wasn't about to push me off a cliff again. He was a loose cannon and I was the spark that could set him off at any moment.

"You forgot your boots," Hayden finally said, making me jump as he broke the long silence.

"What?" I asked.

"Your boots," he repeated slowly.

He held up my brown cowboy boots then tossed them over to me on the bed just as the room grew cold and the snow somehow began to fall in the space completely hidden from the sky.

"You brought them for me?" I asked suspiciously, feeling my eyes grow heavy.

This didn't match up with the evil, murderous Hayden I had just been having a mental fight with. Of course he could have been trying to earn my trust again, just so he could force me off another cliff… though this time I was sure he wouldn't catch me.

"You can't do the tasks barefoot," he said with a shrug, obviously uncomfortable that I found this gesture so touching.

It was definitely out of character for him, to say the least.

"That was really nice," I told him earnestly, though I was pretty sure my words were beginning to slur together. "It's not bad to be nice, you know," I added.

"I have no idea what you're saying," he said with a laugh, his normally angry face actually looking amused. "I think the sleep is starting to get to you," he said by way of explanation. "You're not making any sense."

It was probably just the snow talking, or my completely exhausted brain, but Hayden was becoming more and more difficult to pin down by the second. It would have made much more sense if he had continued to ignore me until the snow came. But now he was suddenly joking with me.

I was starting to feel like the tasks weren't the only impossible things to figure out in this afterlife.

CHAPTER 10

It was odd to me that every morning when I woke from my forced sleep, I couldn't remember my dreams from the night before. I had been a notoriously bad sleeper when I was alive. Most of the time it was terrible to never get a good night's sleep, but the silver lining was the fact that I could always remember my dreams from the restless nights.

In this place, however, there were no dreams and I had to wonder if I had just been sleeping better, or if the dead didn't dream for some reason.

I supposed my existence thus far in the afterlife had been dreamlike in and of itself. Maybe because of the fantastical places I was visiting daily, my mind didn't have the energy to try to top the landscapes I'd been experiencing.

I let this thought echo through my mind while staring up at the dark earth ceiling. A few small roots could be seen coming through the dirt and I thought about just how lovely it would be to stay here forever. I could hang old mason jars with candles in them from the roots on the ceiling, carve whatever I wanted into the walls, then completely wipe them clean and start all over again depending on whatever my whim happened to be at that particular moment.

The entire room smelled just like running through the sprinklers in the summertime and I wasn't anxious to get out of bed, damp and dirty as it may be, to start another impossible task with an impossible man. Hayden seemed to be the only thing that could dampen my mood.

The mud I had stained down my front the day before was now gone and my dress was, once again, spotless white. My hair was remarkably untangled when I knew for a fact if I let the wavy tresses endure wind, water, and nearly falling off a cliff a few times without brushing it, I'd basically have dreadlocks by this point in time. But by some miracle, the afterlife was proving to be very beneficial on the more vain aspects of my personality.

I wasn't about to complain.

Without warning, a knock came at the door, causing me to jump as Hayden entered the room, looking just as annoyed as ever.

"You're still sleeping?" He asked incredulously, his British accent thicker than usual. "Do you know how long I've been waiting for you out there?"

"Good morning to you too," I replied, getting out of bed and putting my cowboy boots back on.

The boots Hayden had retrieved for me.

I still wasn't too sure what to make of him and his constantly changing moods, but I did recognize the fact that this small act of kindness hinted at someone who actually still possessed a soul. He may have been gruff and awful, but I was determined to get the good out of him one way or another. Besides, it had to be better for him stuck in this place if he wasn't so angry all the time. It would make the time go by much faster if he would smile every decade or so.

"Can we just get on with this?" he asked, raising an eyebrow at me lazily in a devil-may-care way.

He had the ability to look both bored and condescending at the same time. It was amazing and frustrating.

"Lead the way," I said, gesturing to the door.

He sighed deeply and exited the room with me following close behind him. As we climbed the stairs I was shocked by the lights streaming down the passageway.

"No fog today?" I asked.

"It's resting higher than normal for some reason so the sun is shining through a bit better."

I tried to think of what this could possibly mean in a place where the weather was so perfectly controlled throughout every cycle. Did that mean I was getting closer to my Destination? Or was it just a coincidence? The sun would always shine for a moment right when I woke up, but by the time Hayden arrived, it would always disappear behind the fog.

Surfacing from the underground room in the tree trunk, I was met by a breathtaking sight. Every task environment I'd seen so far seemed to be more beautiful than the previous, but this one had to top them all.

The tall tree with the purple stone in the trunk was now residing in the middle of a field of brightly-colored tulips. The rows of flowers alternated colors every so often and created a vibrant rainbow that sprawled on endlessly. The mixture of the sun in the thin fog seemed to turn everything gold and caused the flowers themselves to glow from the inside out.

It was stunning to say the least.

"This is beautiful," I said breathlessly.

My eyes were wide with wonder and I couldn't seem to turn around fast enough to catch the beauty from every possible angle.

"Not bad," Hayden agreed with a tight lipped nod.

He had *almost* complimented me.

"Your grandma was Dutch and always kept paintings of tulips around her house. This one was your favorite," he said, reciting my memories once more and surprising me to no end.

"You're such a show off," I told him, rolling my eyes towards the magnificent orange sky.

There were no mountains, only a few hills in the endless field of flowers, though a small cottage could be seen a long ways off. If that was our safe house it didn't really look like there were many obstacles for me to face. At least I wouldn't have to deal with any cliffs or high places in this task. Maybe it was supposed to be an endurance test and I'd just have to stay sane on the walk to the cottage while Hayden threw rude comments at me.

The two of us walked side by side and I let my hand gently graze the top of the tulips as we passed through them. They bobbed lazily back and forth at my touch.

It was actually quite a peaceful stroll and if I tried really hard, I could imagine that I was still alive and taking a romantic walk with some boy I'd met at the bookstore in Greenville.

Maybe I'd been reading books about vocal performance and he'd made some joke about everybody in the south wanting to be a country singer. I'd smile and say I was more folk than country, and he'd ask me if that meant I carried a banjo around with me.

And then I'd come back to reality and remember that I was dead and Hayden wouldn't joke around with me about banjos if his life depended on it.

He might try to kill me with a banjo, but that was another worry all together.

"So what is this third task supposed to be? Walking?" I asked, looking over at my Guide expectantly and hoping he wouldn't say it was some impossible obstacle course where the tulips were about to come to life and eat me.

Hayden stopped walking for a moment and turned to face me. He opened his mouth to speak then stopped suddenly, gasping and opening his eyes wide.

"What?" I asked urgently, looking behind me.

The look on his face suggested that we were suddenly being attacked by some malicious entity, but searching the space behind me I couldn't see any threat.

I turned back to him once more only to see him grasping at his shoulder where a metallic rod was protruding, covered in his blood.

"What is that?" I asked in a frightened whisper.

"Arrow," he responded, his voice tight and strained. "Nice imagination," he added accusatorially.

I walked around him to view the long shaft of an arrow sticking out of his back, moving as he breathed in and out.

Hayden had been shot… by an arrow… in the middle of a tulip field.

If each task was something from my own memory how had this happened? There were definitely no arrows in my grandma's tulip painting.

I looked around frantically, knowing that arrows didn't just shoot themselves. Someone had to be near us and I wasn't about to get an arrow through my heart when I'd already had to endure dying in a car crash and putting up with Hayden for two days.

"Can you walk?" I asked him, facing him and putting my hand on his uninjured shoulder.

I still kept my guard up, scanning the completely empty field for some sign of an attacker. But as little sense as it made, there was no one to be found. Hayden and I were completely alone.

"No," he managed to gasp, before falling to his knees right in front of me.

He grimaced painfully, closing his eyes tight and resting his head against my stomach. It was a pretty vulnerable move for someone so bent on being perceived as tough, and the fact that it was Hayden made me extremely uncomfortable. I didn't mind the actual physical contact of the situation, but seeing someone so strong suddenly become so exposed, frightened me. The situation must have been pretty grim.

Not knowing what to do I placed my hands on his head, stroking his hair and trying to be soothing on the outside while I was completely freaking out on the inside. A million thoughts were passing through my head and Hayden wasn't doing much to help the situation.

I had to know if more arrows were coming. That would tell me if I should be trying to run and get Hayden out of there, or if I had time to sit and try to save him. I also needed to know just how serious his condition was. What did I do if my Guide died?

"Hayden?" I asked, lifting his chin up to face me.

I was instantly shocked by just how terrible he looked. His face was sweaty, his eyes clouded over, and his normally tan skin was now pale and splotched with yellow patches. It was much worse than being impaled by an arrow. There had to be some sort of poison on the tip. I'd seen Daddy hunt enough to know this wasn't a normal reaction.

"Hayden, you have to stay awake so I can help you. We need to get out of here in case they attack again," I said slowly, holding his cheeks to force him to look at me.

It wasn't really doing much good since his eyes kept fluttering closed.

"Hayden?" I said again, trying to get his attention.

"Welcome to Task 3," he breathed, his voice so weak that it frightened me.

Before he passed out completely, he uttered one more sentence: "Reasoning under pressure."

CHAPTER 11

"Hayden!" I shouted, but it was useless.

His body had gone completely limp and he was now sitting on his knees, slumped up against my legs.

"Reasoning under pressure," I repeated. "I just have to get Hayden to safety. That's easy. Not a big deal at all."

I wasn't really buying the false logic that I was repeating aloud in the hopes that it would become true, but it didn't hurt to try. I knew I needed to get Hayden to the safe house somehow. I just hoped we didn't get shot by any more arrows and I could, by some means, heal him.

There was probably medicine in the safe house, hence why it was called a "safe" house. If I could just lug Hayden there in time, I could get him better and be done with the task.

Really, minus the pressure of Hayden dying because I didn't get him where he needed to be in time, this task was the least difficult of the ones I'd faced so far.

Okay fine, the possibility of Hayden's imminent death was pretty motivating, even if he'd always been horrible to me. In his defense he hadn't been *too* rude to me yet since I'd seen him that morning. So he was making progress.

Deciding I probably needed to get down to business, I hooked my arms under Hayden's and lifted with all of my might, trying to get him back on his knees so I could remove the arrow. I propped him up, holding his head to my stomach once more to stabilize him while my free hand grasped the arrow tightly.

Luckily the arrowhead was shaped more like a bullet than a triangle and didn't have any jagged edges to cause damage on the way back out.

"Sorry, Hayden," I said, before closing my eyes and yanking the arrow out.

In all honestly, it was probably better that he was completely out or he wouldn't have been very happy with me for that.

Blood began to ooze from his injury and I instantly had to wonder if removing the arrow had been a good move. I wasn't a doctor by any means and though it had seemed like a good idea at the time, the liquid quickly staining his black shirt suggested otherwise.

"I need to get you some medicine," I said, looking at the safe house over my shoulder.

I could get to the medicine faster if I left Hayden here and ran to and from the safe house without him. But he also might get attacked again, which would definitely be a bad thing. Or he might get worse and I wouldn't be there to help him. I definitely couldn't have that. As it was, while I stood there trying to figure out what I would do, his face had gotten paler and his skin colder.

"Hang on, Hayden," I said, trying to ignore the blood soaking his shirt.

I rolled him over onto his back, hooked him under the arms, and dragged him backwards the best I could. It was slow going and we were leaving a path of broken and destroyed tulips in our wake, but we weren't getting shot at anymore so that was a definite improvement.

It had to take a good fifteen minutes to drag Hayden to the house and by the time we got there I was red in the face and sweaty. Go figure the day the sun would finally show through a bit was the day I had to do hard physical labor.

I wiped the back of my hand across my forehead and dropped my cargo, accidentally hitting Hayden's head on the ground in the process.

"Sorry!" I said with a wince.

Yeah, it was definitely a good thing he wasn't awake for this. He'd murder me for manhandling him so much. In my defense, he had sat by and watched as the stupid zombie from the first task had dropped me on my head.

I could still feel the bump there, even now.

Opening the wooden door to the cottage, I lugged Hayden in with me and grabbed a pillow for him since the concrete floor probably wouldn't be very easy on his already hurt head. Once I'd taken care of him, I searched the few cupboards of the only room in the building for medicine.

"This can't be happening," I thought aloud, closing the last cupboard dejectedly. "How does the safe house not have medicine? What was the point of this task?"

Shaking my head in confusion I walked back over to Hayden, who now looked as if he were gone completely. His skin was ashen and cold, his pulse was faint, and his breathing shallow. It wasn't looking good and if I couldn't figure something out quickly, he'd be dead and it would be all my fault.

"Reasoning under pressure," I said, hoping that by repeating Hayden's words I'd know what to do. "If this all comes from my memory then I must know what to do in this situation. I just have to remember."

I knelt on the hard ground next to Hayden, placing my hand over his wound and closing my eyes. As much as I didn't like him, I definitely couldn't let him die.

If the arrow really was poisoned, I probably should have tried to get the poison out of his blood stream a long time ago. Now the idea of sucking it out like a snake bite seemed almost futile but I had to give it a shot anyway. I knew I'd never forgive myself if someone died because I hadn't tried every possible method to save them.

Leaning over Hayden, I ripped his black T-shirt from the neck, to the hole where the arrow had pierced it. There wasn't as much blood as I had expected but the wound didn't look good.

"Do I cut it or something?" I asked the empty room.

I tried to remember seeing snake bites on movies. It seemed like the hero always cut a little "X" into the helpless woman's skin before sucking the poison out, and if it was in a movie it had to be true, right?

Kidding.

But I had no other plan in mind, so listening to movies seemed like the best option.

I knew I didn't have a knife but Hayden, with his bad boy façade, might very well carry one, and so I searched through his pockets, my tiny hands trying to find anything knifelike. Of course leave it to Hayden to frustrate me even when he was sleeping by not having the knife I needed.

"Only one option then," I said, looking down at the wound and knowing what I had to do.

I may not have had a knife, but I could still try to suck the poison out, as much as I didn't want to.

"Just close your eyes and do it," I told myself, knowing it would be slightly less than pleasant to put my mouth over a bloody wound. But I wouldn't go around fainting at the sight of blood. I'd be logical and resourceful and brave, even if I didn't feel like being any of those things at the moment.

Just like cleaning a snake bite, I poured some water from a pitcher over Hayden's wound, then leaned over and tried to suck the poison out. The bitter taste in my mouth let me know I was at least doing something right, even if I had waited a bit too long to begin this process. Really, I was amazed there was still any poison this close to the wound. It should have made its way into the rest of his body by now.

Maybe I had just been granted a do-over from the Purgatory Task Committee… if such a thing existed.

Before long, the taste of the poison was gone and I hoped more than I'd ever hoped for anything that it meant his blood was clear.

Taking the small scrap of his shirt I'd ripped off, I soaked it in water and held it firmly over the now clean wound. I also washed my mouth out about fifty times, knowing I'd never be able to forget that awful memory.

The wound looked pretty good and I tried to tell myself I'd done a good job, but Hayden was still out cold and the skin around the wound was still burning hot. Something wasn't adding up there and so, I tried again to search my memory for any detail that might be helpful in this situation.

I thought back to the painting in my grandma's house. She'd told me all about her Dutch ancestors and the places she'd seen when she went back to her homeland. She told me about how she loved tulips and always had them in her house.

I remembered how she'd tried to teach me to cook stroopwafels but I'd burned myself on the pan.

"I have a plant for that," she'd said wisely.

"Tulips?" I guessed.

"Jewelweed," she'd responded, reaching for the plant in question.

My burn had healed so quickly once she'd crushed up the plant and smoothed it into my skin.

It was an odd, roundabout connection to my current surroundings but maybe, if my mind was creating the entire task to begin with, there might be some jewelweed just waiting to be used.

"I'll be right back, Hayden," I said to my still Guide.

I couldn't let him die. I had to fix him.

Running out to the front of the cottage, I wasn't all that surprised to find a small garden plot with the exact plant I needed in it. Apparently it paid off to actually stay calm and logical in the face of this ridiculous task.

Wasting no time, I grabbed a handful of the plant, ran back to Hayden, and quickly crushed it up to apply to his wound. The bleeding had stopped thankfully but his breathing was still slow and shallow and I began to worry that I'd taken too long to treat him.

I rubbed the poultice over the skin on his chest and back, hoping my memory had served me well, then I waited. I'm not quite sure what I was waiting for since it wasn't likely that the plant would work instantaneously, but I still sat frozen in place, one hand on Hayden's chest and the other resting in my lap.

If this didn't work, I wasn't sure what else to do. I was pretty outdoorsy, but that didn't mean I could cure someone's wounds all of a sudden.

The only sound in the quiet cottage was the sound of Hayden's shallow breathing and my own heartbeat. After a moment, however, his shallow breathing stopped all together.

"Hayden?" I said, my voice tentative as I looked down at him.

His chest was no longer rising and falling and a cold dread crept through my veins.

"Crap!" I exclaimed, getting to my knees and leaning over his lifeless body.

Trying to recall any training I'd received from my hall advisor my freshman year in the dorms, I plugged his nose, tilted his head back, and pressed my lips to his.

Had the situation not been so dire, it would have been a bit awkward being this intimately close to Hayden. As it was, I tried to ignore the fact that our lips were touching and focused on breathing air into his lungs.

I alternated pumping his chest with my fists and blowing air into his mouth for a good few minutes with no result. No matter how little it seemed to be doing, however, I wouldn't give up. What if a few more seconds would have saved him and I'd given up too soon? But I couldn't deny that I was quickly growing more and more fatigued by the minute.

I'd already spent my morning dragging Hayden's lifeless body across a tulip field, and now my shaky arms were just moments from giving out.

I tried to keep going for as long as I could, but after breathing life in to him one last time, my resolve weakened and I simply rested my forehead against his; our cheeks touching and tears beginning to pool in my eyes.

I didn't like Hayden, it was true. He bugged me and said more rude things than nice things, but that didn't change the fact that I had gotten to know him over the last few days. Whether I wanted it to be the case or not, Hayden was sort of a friend now and he was dying right in front of me. There was no way I was heartless enough to not be affected by that.

"I'm sorry," I whispered into his ear, lacing my arms around his neck and keeping my cheek pressed to his. "I'm so sorry."

"You don't have to be sorry," Hayden whispered back, "You're not *that* bad of a kisser."

CHAPTER 12

I instantly pulled away from Hayden, startled by his sudden speech and delighted that he wasn't dead.

"You're okay!" I practically shouted.

"Well I had an arrow stuck in my shoulder just so you could complete a stupid task, so I wouldn't say I'm okay, but I'm alive," he replied, sounding much stronger already than he had before he'd passed out. "Although I am quite troubled to wake up with my shirt torn practically off and a woman draped across my chest."

"About that," I began, realizing just how bad the situation probably looked to him. "I don't think I ever wanted to admit this to you, but I was actually kind of sad when I thought you'd died."

"So you tore my shirt?" he asked, raising a thick eyebrow at me and slowly sitting up.

"I had to clean out the wound," I explained, motioning

towards his shoulder that was currently covered in the plant poultice.

"I can't trust you with anything," he complained.

Hayden wiped the goop away, flicking it onto the ground and, much to my surprise, his wound was now nothing more than an angry red welt on his skin.

"Okay, I knew I was good, but I didn't think I was *that* good," I said, letting my pride get the better of me just for a moment.

Maybe now that I'd actually done something right, Hayden wouldn't think I was such an idiot.

"Don't be so cocky. It wasn't your hillbilly plant recipe that healed me so fast. You did the right thing, but the task is what sped the process up."

He always had to rain on my parade.

The sky was rapidly darkening outside and I wondered how long I had until the snow began to fall. I didn't feel like I had been in the cycle for very long but it was quickly becoming evident to me that the cycle length was based on my progress through the task, not an actual assigned timeframe.

"Your shoulder is still pretty red," I pointed out.

The room was darker now, though the orange tinted sky still shone through the open window and a fire I hadn't noticed before was crackling in the stone fireplace. In this crazy place it was completely possible that the fire had started itself when we had our backs turned. I was quickly learning that the normal rules of life didn't apply once you were dead.

"It'll be fine," he said, shrugging off my concern uncomfortably.

Heaven forbid someone be nice to him.

"Let me see it," I said, scooting closer to him on the floor and pressing my fingers against the shiny skin. "It feels burning hot still!" I exclaimed.

"It's not burning hot; your fingers are just freezing. You have the worst circulation ever," he assessed, trying to play doctor.

"You're so difficult," I said, grabbing his shoulder and pulling him even closer to me.

"What are you doing?" he asked apprehensively.

It was funny to hear him when he was caught off balance. In fact, it was nice to have the tables turned and be the one making him uncomfortable, since he made a point of making my life miserable on a daily basis.

"My mama taught me that your lips don't change temperature like your hands, so this way I'll be able to see if you're actually burning up or if I'm just cold," I explained, now pressing my lips against the skin on his shoulder.

"Oh, I forgot that's what they taught me in medical school. Kiss the patient's shoulder to make sure they don't have an infection," he mocked, his voice a bit shaky.

I could feel goose bumps spring up on Hayden's arm that I held, but ignored it, trying not to be too proud of my victory. It wasn't every day that you got to put a smug, overly confident man in his place with a few feminine wiles.

Okay… "feminine wiles" was pretty generous. Mostly he was probably just uncomfortable if *anyone* touched him, but I was still happy to know that unshakeable Hayden could be made uncomfortable so easily.

"Are you done yet?" he asked, heaving a deep sigh beneath my lips.

I pulled away, satisfied that I had both taken his temperature, and made him significantly uncomfortable.

"Yes I'm done, you big baby. And I think you'll live. My hands are just cold."

"Like I said," he answered smugly.

I made a face at him but didn't say anything, standing from the floor and getting a better look at the small room now that I wasn't panicked about Hayden dying.

Just like the previous two safe houses, this room had a rocking chair, a bed, a few cupboards, and a fireplace. It seemed like there had to be a reason that every room looked exactly the same on the inside, despite how different each safe house looked externally. Maybe there was some long forgotten memory from my past that made me feel safe in a one room shack.

I was sure Hayden could tell me exactly what memory had created these safe houses, but I wasn't about to ask him and give him the satisfaction of knowing yet another thing that I didn't know.

"You look like a murderer," he pointed out, nodding to my blood-stained white dress.

I didn't say anything to his accusation but shrugged my shoulders noncommittally. It didn't matter what my dress looked like now, it would miraculously clean itself before the start of the next cycle anyway.

Hayden joined me and stood up from the floor as well but quickly brought his hand to the back of his head.

"What did you do to me?" he asked, touching the bump gingerly then wincing at the sensation.

"I might have accidentally dropped you once or twice," I admitted.

"Once or *twice*?" he repeated incredulously.

"It's not my fault," I protested. "If you didn't weigh so much, it wouldn't have been so hard to drag you through that stupid tulip field!"

"I thought you love tulips," he pointed out, pulling from another one of my memories no doubt.

It really wasn't fair that he knew so much about me when I didn't know a thing about him.

"I *loved* tulips," I corrected. "After dragging a mean, unconscious man through them for so long, they kind of lose their appeal. Besides, I still have a bump on my head from that awful zombie from the first task, so you can't really complain about your one small bump."

"Wait," Hayden said, looking like he was actually concerned. "You still have a bump on your head?"

I was taken aback by his reaction. Surely Hayden didn't care if I had a small bump on my head. Heck, he had almost given me worse injuries than that just for fun.

"Yeah… is that important?" I asked.

"You should be… how do I put this? You should be 'resetting' after every cycle," he explained.

"Is that why my dress is never dirty when I wake up?" I asked.

"Leave it to a woman to care more about her dress than her actual health," he scoffed, walking behind me. "Let me see."

Hayden gathered my long hair around my neck and moved it over one shoulder, lacing his fingers through the wavy strands at my scalp gently.

"I'm sure it's not too serious," he said quietly, startlingly close to me with his chest pressed against my back.

His fingers searched over my scalp, finding the bump and sending a stinging pain through my head.

"Ouch!"

"Now who's being the baby?" he teased.

He pressed around the bump a few times before untangling his hands from my hair and moving them from my scalp, down my neck, and finally resting them on my bare shoulders for a moment. I hadn't realized how cold my skin was until Hayden's warm hands pointed out the difference in our temperatures.

Now I know I said he was awful and rude and had a temper and I couldn't stand him… but I'd be lying if I didn't become instantly aware of the fact that Hayden and I were standing very close together, and he was extremely attractive (when he didn't open his mouth to speak). Really though, who could blame me for wishing he was the boy in my daydream, who liked to joke around and compliment me?

Neither of us spoke and I had to wonder why he kept his hands on my shoulders. I wished I could see his face to read his expression, but if I turned around now, I knew our little moment would be broken; and it was the first nice moment we'd had since meeting each other. I had to take full advantage of that. It wasn't like I got a lot of time at the end of the day to sit and think about my experiences with him.

The snow fell and I slept.

It may have been the most effective sleep aide ever but it also left me no time to recuperate at the end of each cycle.

His thumb ran across my collar bone just for a moment before he pulled away all together, clearing his throat and breaking whatever spell had fallen over us.

"The bump isn't that bad," he said, sounding odd. "I'm not sure why it isn't healing, but if you stop whining about it I'm sure it'll go away."

I turned to face him, still distractingly close. He looked down at me in a way that was meant to be strong an intimidating, but somewhere in his scowl, I could see that he was hiding behind his sarcasm and insults.

"What, are you a doctor now?" I asked him with a

small laugh, lightening the mood.

"Personal question," he said simply, turning away from me and sitting in the rocking chair; his self-proclaimed spot.

I went to lay down on the bed just as I always did, ready for the snow to fall and sleep to take me.

"I almost forgot about your aversion to mixing business with real life," I said, feeling quite put out by the lack of balance in our knowledge.

Even though he was completely crazy and had random outbursts of rage, I had grown to trust Hayden (as much as I could trust a crazy person). It didn't seem fair that I'd had to build that trust without knowing anything about him, yet he didn't trust me one bit and he knew everything he could ever want to know about me. All he had to do was somehow pull the knowledge from my memory that he had full access to; without my permission might I add.

"I don't suppose you're ever going to tell me who you are?" I pressed, hoping I could get something out of him.

"I'm your Guide," he said stiffly.

I'd lost him.

We'd had a nice moment and now he was back to being closed off and keeping me safely at bay. Still, it was nice to not be alone. No matter how stiff the company was.

"Sorry you had to get shot for me to complete my task," I said after a moment.

Hayden let out a little laugh, still staring into the fire and not looking at me.

"Yeah, I don't know how that ended up being fair, but I guess if it motivated you then it was worth it," he replied, still laughing softly.

"It was weird," I began. "I didn't see anyone out in that field who could have shot you. I swear we were completely alone."

"Of all the odd things that little imagination of yours has come up with, I think that is the least of your worries."

I nodded in agreement. I still wasn't convinced that I was responsible for these odd and breathtaking landscapes we found ourselves in every morning, but I'd take credit for it if Hayden really wanted to give it to me.

"Any idea what we'll be facing tomorrow?" I asked, closing my eyes as a few cold white flakes fell on my cheek bones, tickling my skin.

"No, but I can only hope it doesn't involve me getting shot again. Thanks for that, by the way."

"Anything for you, Hayden," I joked. "Still, as unpleasant as you are, I am sad to see you go."

I wasn't sure where these words were coming from and

honestly, I wished I could stop them, but the snow was making me tired and my roommate Monica could attest to the fact that I said some crazy things when I was tired.

“Thank you for that backhanded compliment,” he answered, sounding much closer to me than he had been before.

I opened my eyes to see him standing over the bed looking at me with a bemused expression.

“You know, I think ‘tired Isla’ is my favorite. She doesn’t whine as much.”

“You’re the worst,” I informed him with a smile, just as my lids drooped closed one final time.

CHAPTER 13

I seemed to wake to a new sensation at the beginning of every cycle. For the ill named motor skills task it had been the sun on my face. With the reasoning under pressure task it had been the smell of wet earth. Today, however, the first thing I noticed was slightly unpleasant and more than a little panic-inducing.

As with the beginning of every cycle, it was sunny outside, for just a moment. Of course, in the time it took me to notice that the sun was streaming in between the slats of the window, it had already disappeared behind the thick fog. But today, a loud metallic screeching could be heard outside of the cottage.

I wasn't sure I really wanted to investigate something that sounded actively sinister since my last few tasks had proven difficult enough without the added pressure of some deadly machine. I could only imagine what that sound meant for me.

"Isla? You'd better not be sleeping still," Hayden called through the door, not even bothering to knock before he opened it.

I would have been more offended but I guessed there wasn't much for him to walk in on. It wasn't like I needed to change my clothes every morning, or even bathe. The perks of being dead definitely included clean clothes, a clean start every morning, and no need to eat or drink. It was kind of like being indestructible, though the bump on the back of my head did quite a bit to overturn that comparison.

Still, it was nice going through a task where you had to scale the side of a floating island when you didn't have to worry about taking a bathroom break halfway through.

Talk about added pressure.

"Morning," I said, trying to look over Hayden's shoulder to see what might be in store for me.

"Are you ready to begin the task?" he asked, sounding like any progress I might have made the night before in getting through his tough exterior was wasted. He was all business again, as usual.

"You know, just because I'm technically sleeping in between tasks doesn't mean I get much of a mental break from all of this. It isn't really fair that I get just a few minutes at the end of every task to unwind. It's exhausting," I told him.

"You were just sleeping. You're fine," he answered simply, not having any sympathy for me apparently.

"Not physically, Hayden," I said with a sigh. "It's mentally exhausting. It's like I do a task, blink my eyes, and suddenly it's time for the next task with no cool-down time in between."

"I'm glad we've started today off with you whining already. I was worried we wouldn't have time to fit that into this task."

"You try constantly performing without any rest," I mumbled, mad that he wasn't giving me the sympathy I wanted.

"Trust me, what I do is worse," he replied, making me wonder, not for the first time, what he did when I was "sleeping".

Of course I didn't bother asking him since I knew it was completely useless to try to get any information out of him that didn't have to do with whatever task I'd be performing that day.

"Let's go then," I said, lifting my shoulder then dropping it heavily in defeat.

“You’re chipper.”

I didn’t say anything to his remark, knowing he was just trying to get under my skin. Instead, I left the cabin to survey the surroundings of my next task. I could only hope it would be as pretty as the ones before it since the scenery was a small compensation for how awful each task turned out to be.

If I was expecting tulip fields and beautiful floating islands I was sorely disappointed when I walked straight into a pile of trash and scrap metal.

The metallic screeching grew louder though I still couldn’t locate its source.

“What is this place?” I asked in disgust.

Hayden smiled over at me.

“Don’t look at me, you’re the one with the dirty mind,” he answered with a laugh, apparently very proud of his joke.

I guessed when you made one joke every year or two you’d have to really enjoy it.

I rolled my eyes at his attempted humor and picked my way through the endless piles of garbage. It didn’t seem possible that it could keep going but from what I could tell, the refuse went on forever.

It piled up high above me and sprawled out endlessly.

More than anything it resembled a big city full of sky scrapers that all happened to be made from discarded car parts and old toasters. The foggy air looked brown and dirty, and there wasn't one spec of greenery to be found.

"I can't believe this really came out of my mind," I said, curling my lip up at the rust that surrounded me. Already, my white lace dress had a few crimson rust streaks along the sides where I'd brushed against piles of scrap.

"Not one of your best inventions," Hayden agreed. "Which reminds me, Task four: Ingenuity."

"Ingenuity?" I repeated, looking at my surroundings and feeling like I understood where this was going. "So I need to build something?"

"Two somethings," Hayden corrected. "One thing to get you to the safe house up there," he began, pointing to a little office building at the top of one of the trash piles.

"And the other?" I asked, thinking I probably didn't want the answer to this inquiry.

"The other is up to you. But you'll probably want to make sure it can stop that," he said with a nod over my shoulder.

I didn't really want to turn around to see what he was talking about. I was sure it was the source of the screeching noise and probably something I'd have to face. Instead I continued to look at Hayden.

"And I suppose you won't be helping me at all?"

"Have I helped you in any of the other tasks?" he asked rhetorically.

"Point taken."

"Well then, if you don't have any questions I'll just leave you to it."

And with that, I blinked my eyes and he was gone.

I wasn't quite sure where he'd gone or how he'd left but I supposed it didn't really matter. What mattered was that I was alone and there was something behind me that I'd need to defeat.

Mustering what little courage I had, I turned around to properly survey my task.

A ways away was something that looked like a large metallic spider. Its long spindly legs bent in odd places that made it walk with a bit of a limp, but it still moved quickly, looking lethal. Its body looked like a rusty yellow bumper car from a carnival I had visited when I was little, and I had to wonder if this was a mix of different memories all merging together into one big, rusty mess.

Though this creature was troubling, the most alarming thing about it was the two pinchers it held in front of its body. Like its legs, they were made from long metal pieces, but on the end of both poles rested two circular saws, whirring quickly and cutting through the piles of metal that blocked the spider's path with a loud screech.

At least that explained the noise.

"Fantastic," I breathed sarcastically.

I guess compared to zombies, death by saw would be a lot quicker and less painful, right? Like I said, I could be logical.

"Okay Tuck, what would you do?" I asked, wishing my big brother was there to help me out.

He was nothing if not an inventor and I was sure he'd be able to look around and create something amazing in a matter of minutes. As it was, I was on my own and completely hopeless as the spider came closer and closer to me.

I wasn't really sure if it had seen me yet, but since its sole purpose in life was to motivate me to build something so that it couldn't kill me, I didn't doubt it knew I was there. Maybe it was biding its time to give me a fair start.

"The only way to get rid of it would be to smash it," I reasoned, acting like it was a real spider and not a huge metallic death machine. "But anything heavy enough to smash it would be too heavy for me to pick up, so that doesn't really work."

I twirled my white-blonde hair around my finger absent-mindedly, actually being very calm in the face of almost certain second death. Panicking wouldn't really get me anywhere; I knew that, and so I kept my breathing even as I surveyed the area for any possible parts I could use to kill the machine.

A few trash piles away I could see a car suspended in midair by some sort of giant magnet. If I could somehow manage to cut the chain holding the car while the spider was underneath it, I could easily destroy it. Cutting through a thick chain didn't really seem possible though, and I wouldn't really have to invent anything to do it.

I thought back on Hayden's instructions and wondered if it was really necessary to *invent* something, or if simply being innovative with the materials around me would be enough to show my ingenuity. I didn't want to risk failing the task just because I'd bent the rules a bit, but at the same time, I wasn't an inventor. My brother Tuck had always been good with building things and creating new machines out of parts from old ones, but that was a talent I sadly hadn't inherited.

"Are you trying to fail on purpose or do you just want to bug me?" Hayden asked, right next to my ear, causing me to jump about a mile in the air.

"What are you doing here?" I asked, slightly breathless from his unexpected ambush.

He smirked at me, his full lips tugging up in one corner.

"I got bored," was his simple reply. "Plus you were just standing here and I thought maybe you'd been scared stiff."

"Oddly enough, I'm very calm right now," I told him.

Of course I didn't bring up the fact that I was slightly resigned to my death at this point since I couldn't think of a single way to stop the spider from cutting me in half.

"So brave," he joked.

It was odd to hear him joking around with me rather than berating me for being weak or slow. Maybe I had broken down his walls at least a little. Fat lot of good it did me though since I was about to die again.

"Let's say I don't invent something, per se," I began tentatively, watching his reaction. "What if I just utilize what I have around me… but in a clever way?"

"I don't think I'd be relying on your cleverness or cunning if I were you," he said, sounding like the Hayden I knew and… not loved… maybe tolerated.

"Did you come here to make my job more difficult?" I

asked.

“I came down here to ensure that *you* didn’t fail and give me a losing track record.”

“But you can’t help me,” I pointed out.

“Glad you listened to at least one thing I’ve told you,” he said sounding very put out. “And no, I can’t help you. But I can offer some moral support and very subtly inform you that the crane holding up that car you were eyeing, is still in working order.”

“Well, Hayden Smith,” I said in surprise, making up a last name for him. “If I didn’t know any better I’d say you were offering your help.”

“Temple,” he said.

“What?”

“Hayden Temple.”

“And you’re giving out personal information. I never thought I’d see the day.”

I smiled too sweetly over at him, being overly dramatic in my praise.

“Do you want my help, or do you want to die again?” he asked, obviously fed up with my little act.

“I’d rather not die again,” I said. “If it’s not too inconvenient for you.”

“Oh trust me; it’s monumentally inconvenient for me.

But I'm your Guide so I'm forced to do what I can for you."

"Except help me."

"Except that," he agreed, closing his eyes and nodding.

We were both startled out of our little exchange by the sound of the machine looming ever closer, effectively cutting a VW Bus in half as it crawled towards us.

"Now, I don't mean to judge your method when I'm trying to be supportive," Hayden began.

"But?"

"But, shouldn't you actually be doing something?"

"Oh fine, you kill joy," I said with a laugh.

I wasn't sure what I found so funny about the whole situation. In all honesty, it was more likely that I'd fail this task than succeed, but having someone there to talk to and joke around with made the experience infinitely better. It must have been all of the horrible things Hayden had said to me during the other tasks that now made me so easy to please. He didn't even have to be nice to me anymore. If he just refrained from saying something jerky I was beyond happy with him.

"I need to get the machine under that car so I can smash him," I explained, picking my way through the rubble towards the vehicle, suspended in midair.

“Smash him? You make it sound like you’re figuring out how to kill a bug in your shower,” Hayden answered.

“Trust me, if I found a bug in my shower, that thing would be dead before it knew what hit it.”

“Besides that, I’m not sure how much ‘luring’ you’ll need to do since the monster is obviously after you,” he added, completely ignoring my statement.

“But how do I get it to stay under the car if I’m up in the cab of the… what would you call it? A crane?”

“Sure.”

“I can’t operate the crane or it’ll come up there after me. And *you* certainly can’t operate it because that would count as helping me,” I reasoned.

It didn’t look like I’d be finding a way around this task any time soon. I could only be grateful the spider had started off so far away from me, that way I had time to think things through as it approached.

“That is a problem,” Hayden agreed.

Of course it shouldn’t have surprised me that he was offering no suggestions to get me out of this mess. But that didn’t mean it had to bug me any less.

Stopping underneath the old rusty car that dangled from the giant circular magnet, I thought of any possible way to be in two places at once.

"You know, I think you're over complicating things," Hayden remarked, sounding bored.

I guess it was easy to be bored when you didn't have your life on the line.

"Would you stop talking?" I hissed, closing my eyes and concentrating.

It was obvious to me that I needed to stand under the car in order to get the spider right where I wanted it. Somehow I'd need to access the controls within the crane's cab to drop the car at just the right moment. But that also meant I'd not only have to access the controls from where I stood outside of the cab, but I'd also have to make sure I got out from under the car before it fell.

I didn't really have *that* much faith in my speed.

Running over to the crane's cab I hopped in and began examining the console. Luckily, from my vantage point under the car I'd be able to see all of the buttons, even if I was too far away to do anything with that advantage.

"The big red one says 'magnet'," Hayden pointed out.

"I guess it's not considered helping when you're pointing out the obvious?" I asked in annoyance. "Doesn't matter if I know where the button is if I can't reach it from under the car. If the cab of the crane weren't so far away…"

"I don't think this is really considered a crane."

"You think I care about what it's called when that stupid spider machine is about to kill me?" I asked rhetorically, hopping back out of the cab and wildly searching the ground for anything that might be useful.

A few feet away I was able to find something that resembled half of a metal hula hoop. Grinning to myself I snatched it up and examined it.

"What is that thing?" Hayden asked.

"I think it's one of those things that holds a canopy above your bed… well… half of it anyway."

"Half a canopy?"

"Half of the holder," I answered, giving him an exasperated look to show him I was not amused by his little jokes. "Now stop asking stupid questions. I know you can't help me, but that doesn't mean you should be hindering me either."

An idea beginning to form in my mind I dropped to my knees on the ground, searching with quick hands through the piles of trash until I found what I was looking for.

"Blinds?" he asked as I picked up the window shade.

"I don't need the blinds," I explained. "Just the plastic turner on them."

I pulled the item in question off of the blinds, glad to

see that the attachment on the end of the long plastic shaft was still intact, giving me a notch at the end of the plastic that I could use.

"Look for another one of these," I instructed Hayden.

He gave me a skeptical look, obviously wondering if this was helping me and I'd suddenly be disqualified.

"I figured everything out myself, I just need you to find this," I said, trying to justify it.

Hayden didn't say anything, he simply raised a thick eyebrow at me, still not willing to break the rules.

For a bad boy look alike, he was kind of square.

"Ugh, fine!" I sighed, searching the junkyard for what I was looking for. "There!" I called, seeing one next to Hayden. "Can you at least pull it off of the rest of the blinds for me?"

"You ask so much," he sighed, doing as I asked and handing the long plastic piece over to me. "And what is this supposed to accomplish again?"

"I'm completing the task," I answered simply.

Walking over to Hayden, I grabbed the waist of his pants and tugged him towards me, startling him quite a bit as his brow furrowed.

"Dang it," I said, disappointed at the lack of stretch in his black pants.

"Love, this is hardly the time or the place," he said very seriously, giving me his version of a seductive smile.

It was more effective than he knew.

"You're disgusting," I informed him. "That is definitely not what I was going for. I just need some elastic or something."

"Sure," he said somberly, sounding like he pitied my nonexistent infatuation with him.

"And for the record, that's *never* going to be what I meant."

"Thank goodness."

I didn't dignify his statement with a response. With the metallic screeching of the spider now startlingly close to me, I attempted to find the last missing piece of my invention. Of course, this invention largely relied on my aim, which was quite rusty from lack of practice.

"Finally," I whispered to myself, spotting what appeared to be pajama pants lying on top of an old refrigerator.

Needless to say, I didn't waste any time pulling the elastic band from the waist of the pajamas. I ran back over to my mark beneath the dangling car and constructed my very rough bow and arrows, hoping that I would be able to hit such a small target from so far away.

"I can understand what you're doing," Hayden began. "I just can't understand how you think you'll be able to hit the button in one shot while worrying about being torn to shreds by a saw."

"Thank you for painting that colorful picture for me," I called to him.

Of course Hayden was stationed safely next to the cab of the crane, keeping himself well out of the way of danger. He was infuriating to say the least.

I could feel the ground rumble beneath my feet as the spider approached behind me. My focus was trained on the button that would save me from this task, and the fact that I had to hit it with a blind turner, an elastic string, and half a bed canopy didn't inspire much hope. Suddenly the whole idea seemed entirely ridiculous and my knees began to shake.

How on earth was this going to work?

Still, I took my aim, hoping for the best. I looked over my shoulder for just a moment, seeing the spider only a few yards behind me now as the screeching became almost deafening.

The window of time I had to actually hit the button was very small. Somewhere in that window I had to make sure the spider was close enough to crush but not close enough to chop me in half. Not a great prospect, but definitely a great motivator.

"Any time now, Isla," Hayden called, actually looking very worried about me all of a sudden.

It was unexpected, though it did little to actually help me. Still, the idea that he was slightly put out by my possible second death was touching.

"Isla!" he shouted, just as I could feel the heat of the machine on the back of my neck, my hair blowing up around me from the whirring of the saw.

Taking one last deep breath I released the elastic band that held my arrow and watched intently as it flew through the air, striking the cab console just to the left of the red button.

If I'd had time, I would have cursed my bad luck, but as it was, I needed to reload my arrow and try one last time before either dying or making a run for it.

Hayden's face was a mask of pure panic now and though it shouldn't have, it surprised me to see him looking worried. Maybe he just didn't want to be scarred by the bloody scene that would ensue from my failure.

Either way, I put his face out of my mind as I reloaded my "arrow", ignored the whirring blade just one foot from my skin, and shot at my target one final time.

This time the plastic shaft hit the target dead on and I allowed myself one quick smile, proud of my victory. I had actually managed to hit the target from so far away!

The only problem was, even after hitting the button, the car above me didn't budge.

CHAPTER 14

"What?" I mouthed, before a harsh prod in my back sent me sprawling onto the dirty floor.

I yelled out in fear as one of the sharp, metal spider legs penetrated the ground beside me, burrowing deep into the earth.

This was it. I'd failed the task and now the stupid machine was going to rip me to pieces.

I scrambled around on the ground, trying to get to my knees to crawl away before the thing killed me, but another leg came racing down above me, this one pinning the skirt of my dress to the ground.

Knowing I was completely out of luck and hoping death-by-saw wouldn't be too painful, I looked up at Hayden desperately, only to see that he was no longer looking at me. Instead, he was tripping over himself as he lunged at the red button on the console, pressing it down firmly before appearing by my side and yanking me by the wrists away from the spider.

He pulled me backwards so that I came crashing down on top of him and a split second later, the sound of metal on metal could be heard as small pieces of debris flew over us in the gust of wind that followed the chaos. I closed my eyes tightly against Hayden's chest as he shielded my head from the metal pieces that shot off in every direction and suddenly, the air was silent.

I didn't move for a long time. Instead I concentrated on matching the motion of Hayden's chest as it rose and fell, trying to steady my breathing. His hands still rested on my head as a thousand thoughts raced through my mind, though one was more pressing than the others.

Had I failed the task because Hayden had helped me?

After a long while I opened my eyes and lifted my head to get a good look at Hayden. He looked just as shocked as I felt and our blue eyes were wide.

"What happened?" I asked in a whisper.

"I don't know," he answered, his voice betraying how uncomfortable he was with the whole situation.

"Sorry," I said quickly, pushing myself up off of Hayden so I was no longer impairing his breathing.

I sat on the ground next to him, my dress completely

covered in mud and rust and ripped along the bottom from where Hayden had pulled me away from the spider.

The spider!

I turned around quickly, surveying my fallen foe and hoping it didn't have some sort of secret reboot system. Even though I didn't know much about machinery, I could safely say the thing looked beyond repair as it sat smoking beneath the car.

"You saved me," I said to Hayden, trying to keep it from sounding like an accusation, even though it kind of was.

"I didn't," he answered quickly, shaking his head in denial and looking like he might actually regret saving my life.

"You pushed the button."

"I didn't mean to," he emphasized.

He still looked shocked and I wasn't sure what he was more upset about, that he'd broken the rules to save me, or that he might have been caught doing something nice.

"What does this mean?" I asked, scared for the answer. "Do I fail?"

Hayden looked around the junkyard, as if he could see the answer written in the piles of trash.

"I don't think so," he began slowly. "I mean… you

figured out how to kill the thing on your own. You even built something to do it. That was all the task really called for."

He still sounded unsure and I didn't like the uncertainty in his voice when it was my death on the line.

"When will we find out if I failed? Will it be immediately, or do they wait until you've completed all the tasks to finally tell you, 'Oops, sorry! You didn't make it.'," I asked, slightly hysterical now.

"I don't know," Hayden answered, sounding a bit angry.

"What about your cousin? How did it work with her?" I asked.

I felt bad about having to bring her up again. I could tell the topic obviously hurt Hayden, but I had to know if I was completely out of luck now.

He winced at the mention of his first failed attempt to guide someone to their Destination but he answered me nonetheless.

"We knew immediately," he said quietly, staring straight ahead.

I wanted to know what he meant by that but didn't press the issue any further. Just because Hayden had impulsively saved my life didn't mean he had suddenly stopped hating me, and if I wanted to get to my Destination, I needed to stay on his good side.

A breeze blew through the junkyard, throwing up dust as it did so and breaking up the silence between us just slightly. I wasn't sure if I should say anything else or just get up and complete the second part of the task. Hayden was pretty much impossible to read and I never knew when he was being dark and brooding, just ready to blow up at someone, or when he was simply quiet because he had nothing to say.

Eventually I stood up and brushed my dress off; an action that was completely pointless since there was no way I'd ever get the stains out of the white lace… until the cycle reset and I was magically clean again.

This place was so bizarre.

Hayden followed my lead, getting to his feet and running his fingers absently through his dark, messy hair.

"Thank you for saving me," I said finally, looking up at the safe house instead of at Hayden.

He wasn't really the emotional type. I didn't think he'd want me to stare longingly into his eyes while thanking him. Really, giving him any sort of praise for his act of bravery was probably too touchy-feely for him.

"It was nothing," he said gruffly, shrugging off my

compliment as if it were physically painful to be on the receiving end of kindness.

"So now I just need to get to the top of that trash pile?" I asked, pointing up at the safe house that rested high above us.

It may have been very blatantly changing the subject, but I didn't think Hayden would mind too much if it meant I'd stop complimenting him.

"You have to build something to get yourself up there," he corrected.

"I can't just climb?" I whined.

"You can if you want to cut yourself on a rusty piece of metal and get Tetanus."

"Too late for that," I told him, holding out my arm and showing him the bloody cut I had received from the spider's attack.

"You really do have a penchant for getting hurt, don't you?"

He gave one long-suffering sigh and grabbed my arm to examine it. If there was one thing Hayden obviously enjoyed, it was playing doctor. Or maybe he didn't enjoy it; he was just constantly forced into that role because of my clumsiness. He ran his thumb over the wound, effectively smearing blood over my skin and grossing me out all at the same time.

"Shouldn't you not be touching blood with your bare hands?" I asked with a raised eyebrow.

I was just *slightly* skeptical of his nonexistent medical credentials.

"Do you have some sort of disease you aren't telling me about? Besides being chronically annoying?"

"I'll ignore that," I said.

"How generous of you," he responded, still checking out my cut to determine if it was fatal. "Yet again, you've narrowly escaped death with this little paper cut."

"That's a deep cut!" I insisted.

I may have refrained from crying about my wound, but I wasn't about to have this smug man tell me it was nothing. If I'd been home (and alive) Monica would have called in the national guard by now and watched five Youtube videos on how to stitch up a wound using only items found in your kitchen. Just because I wasn't a sobbing mess didn't mean it didn't hurt.

"You're such a baby," he said, releasing my arm, wiping my blood on his pants, and returning his gaze to the safe house that resembled an office building.

When his back was safely turned I made a face at the back of his head but decided not to verbally retaliate.

"How loosely are we using the term 'invent' for this task?" I asked.

"Well seeing as how you 'invented' a bow and arrow… which has definitely already been invented, I'd say the term is ill-used in this context."

"Perfect," I said with a smile.

I didn't know what I could possibly invent to get me up to the safe house, but I was sure I could build some sort of pulley system, or rock climber-ish mechanism. That wasn't beyond reason.

"I'd ask if you have any ideas, but I know you can't help me," I said.

"Nope."

"Except for five minutes ago when you *did* help me."

"Mhm."

Apparently that was all I'd get out of him on that subject, though he wasn't getting off that easily. I'd be revisiting Hayden's little deviation from the rules once we'd completed this task.

Until the snow came.

Stupid rules.

"See you up there then?" he asked, not waiting for me to respond.

Before I could turn my head to look at him he was

gone. If there was one thing to be said about Hayden, it was that he didn't overstay his welcome.

I sighed deeply before returning to the task at hand. Somehow I had to figure out how to get to the top of a cliff… made of garbage… by inventing something. I still couldn't see what any of these tasks had to do with getting to heaven but I wasn't about to fail them and find out where I'd go instead.

The pile of garbage loomed ominously before me but I refused to be intimidated. All I needed was something to toss me up there.

Maybe a catapult of some sort?

With this potentially bad idea in mind, I began searching the area for anything I could possibly use. It didn't take long to find the appropriate materials in the piles of garbage and before long, I was actually starting to construct a crude catapult.

Most of the materials had to be tied together rather than welded or nailed, but the ties seemed to be doing their job so I couldn't be too picky on that front.

"Something tells me you're executing a poorly thought out plan right now," Hayden said, making me jump once more.

"Would you stop doing that?" I shouted.

My nerves were already shot from the task today without Hayden suddenly appearing in front of me, unannounced.

"Stop doing what? Offering my friendly advice?"

"It's fine if you want to stay here, and it's fine if you want to leave, but don't pop in and out like that. It's freaking me out," I told him.

"What are you even doing with that stuff?" he asked, kicking the pile of garbage that immediately fell apart.

"You just ruined my catapult!"

"Catapult?" he repeated skeptically. "You were going to try to launch yourself up to the safe house?"

"Maybe," I answered defensively.

Hayden broke out in uncontrollable laughter at my response, instantly garnering a dirty look from me.

"That's the stupidest thing I've ever heard! Why didn't you just try to build an airplane out of a shoelace?"

Hayden continued to laugh while I continued to stare at him in annoyance. I swear he hadn't left all that long ago. Apparently it didn't take long for him to get bored with waiting for me.

"I hate you so much," I told him, beginning my search once more for something that could help me scale a rusty trash mountain.

"Sticks and stones," he countered.

"What about this?" I asked him, holding up a bright orange, wound up length of extension cord. "Think this could hold my weight?"

Hayden assessed the cord apprehensively, then looked me up and down, making me suddenly self-conscious.

"I wouldn't be willing to bet your life on it."

"That was almost sweet of you," I told him with a little wink, tying the end of the cord to a desk lamp I'd found.

"Grappling hook?" he guessed.

I lifted my shoulder at him then turned to face the pile of trash in front of me. One of these days, when I wasn't fighting my way through bizarre tasks, I'd have time to go back and reflect on what in the world had sparked this particular landscape in my memory. Then I'd work on having it permanently extracted.

"Do you really think you have the arm strength to launch that lamp up to the house?" he asked me.

"I don't need to get it all the way to the house," I replied.

Jutting out of the mountain of junk was something that looked like a metal bed frame. I wasn't sure how sturdy it was, but I had hopes that it would be able to support me as I pulled myself up using the makeshift grappling hook.

"It's a pretty far climb," Hayden pointed out. "Do you really want to put so much faith in something that likely won't hold you?"

There he went; sort of caring again.

It would have been sweet if I'd thought it was motivated by something other than his own selfish desire to get someone to their Destination and clear his previously failing record. Hayden's desire to get me through this, no matter what the motivation, was still very useful, so I didn't let myself feel hurt over the "why" of the situation.

"I guess we'll find out if it works huh?" I asked, pulling my good arm back behind me and using all of my strength to throw the lamp over my head towards the bed frame.

Luckily for me, it overshot the target quite a bit and came falling back down towards me after curving over the metal pole of the frame.

"Even better!" I exclaimed, grabbing the lamp and wrapping the other end of the cord around it, creating a makeshift pulley system.

"Lucky throw," Hayden said from on top of the pile near the safe house.

He was such a show off.

"Be there in a second," I called confidently.

I gave the cord a firm tug to test out its strength. When it didn't budge I jumped up and took hold of it, letting my entire weight rest on it just a foot or two off the ground. The bed frame let out a low metallic groan but yet again, the cord didn't budge and I took that as proof enough that I would be fine using this to climb.

The arm strength required to pull myself up to the safe house would be a bit of a problem, but I figured if I could simply rely on the adrenaline of a possible fall, I might be able to pull it off. Besides, the climb wouldn't be a very long one. I only had to exert myself for a short amount of time.

The dirty fog in the air seemed to cling to my skin as I pulled myself hand over hand up the extension cord. I held myself in a horizontal position as my feet walked up the vertical wall of trash as if it were a sidewalk. I could feel the grime in the air settle over my sweaty forehead and I couldn't wait for the cycle to reset so I could be clean again.

I could only hope the next task would be in a pretty area like the ones before this.

"I'm quite impressed," Hayden called, now only a few feet away from me as I continued on my upward climb.

"You should be," I said breathlessly, my arms shaking

with the effort of keeping me upright.

I didn't dare look back to see how far I'd come or I knew I'd panic and let go of the "rope". Not something I really wanted to do right at that moment.

By the time I reached the end of my rope, both literally and figuratively, I was ready to collapse into a heap. I pulled myself up over the ledge of rusty metal and lay on the ground outside of the safe house for a good few minutes, trying to catch my breath as Hayden stood over me with a smug smile on his face. I wasn't sure what he was so happy about but it was annoying me to no end.

"Tired?" he asked happily.

So that was it? He was happy that I was showing my weakness once more? He just loved any reason to point out any of my shortcomings, which I was quickly learning were numerous.

If nothing else, dying had definitely shown me how out of shape I was.

"It's easy for you to poke fun at me. You just pop up here without any effort," I said, finally getting to my feet and steadying my breathing. "I wish I could watch you complete these tasks while I just stood back and laughed."

"Maybe one day," he said.

"Don't get my hopes up if you can't follow through," I

responded, walking toward the safe house and away from my impossibly frustrating Guide.

CHAPTER 15

The safe house was slightly different from the others in its décor, though the general layout of the room stayed exactly the same. The small room had one bed as usual, though it looked like a hospital bed. Instead of cupboards there were filing cabinets, the rocking chair was metal, and our "fireplace" was a space heater.

"Cozy," I said sarcastically, shuffling my feet over the linoleum floor.

"You created it," Hayden countered once more.

I couldn't argue with him there, no matter how bizarre I thought it was that I had decided to pull a junkyard from my memory over anything else I could have possibly used.

"Why this?" I asked him, nodding up to the flickering fluorescent light overhead.

"I know you think I can read your mind, but you're going to have to be a bit more specific for me."

"Of all the memories I've acquired over the years, why did we end up in a junkyard?" I asked, trying to be "more specific" to discourage anymore snide remarks from my Guide.

Hayden shrugged; something he did often.

"We needed something that made sense as an ingenuity task and this worked I guess," he explained, taking his normal spot in the metal rocking chair while I sat on the paper covered hospital bed.

Not exactly comfortable.

"Oh *we* needed it?" I asked, wondering who the "we" was in this situation. Maybe his super-secret boss? "Who is we?"

Hayden shrugged.

"Would you stop doing that?" I asked in frustration.

"You say that an awful lot."

"And you do an awful lot of frustrating things. You see how this works?"

"The snow can't come soon enough," he stated.

"All I was saying, is that this task was bizarre," I told him, trying to make peace. "The other tasks I can understand. They were pretty and kind of heavenly looking. But this junkyard was out of place. This whole situation is like a movie that doesn't know what it wants to be. One minute it's sci-fi, the next it's horror, and then it's like a bad romantic comedy where I'm stuck with someone who looks like you but is a total jerk."

"Looks like me?" he asked, very plainly puzzled.

I was immediately kicking myself for saying that since the last thing Hayden needed, was the knowledge that he was kind of ridiculously attractive. Up until this point, I had learned that he was otherwise unaware of this fact. And even now, he seemed to not understand what I had said so I ran with it.

"Yeah… because you look like someone who would be nice," I improvised. Very badly might I add.

"It's the accent isn't it?" he asked with a sigh. "I think it's Hugh Grant's fault. You American girls think anyone with an English accent is a well-spoken gentleman who's going to sweep you off your feet."

"Technically you did sweep me off my feet," I began with a grin. "And right over a cliff."

"Details," Hayden replied, waving the issue away with his hand, though I could see a hint of a smile under those stubbly cheeks of his. "Let me see your arm."

I was thrown off by the sudden change in topic, but obliged as he walked over to me to examine my cut.

"You've certainly been more helpful lately," I accused.

"We're getting closer to the end. I figured if you've made it this far, you might actually get to your Destination."

"Which will look good to your mystery boss."

"Yep," he replied, his eyes roaming over my arm expertly.

My cut didn't really hurt too much anymore, but it didn't look like it was getting any better either. The only thing that seemed to heal well in this place was Hayden.

Curious, I grabbed his shoulder with my free hand and pulled him closer to where I sat on the hospital bed. I tugged the no-longer-torn neck of his shirt down to see that the injury he'd sustained in the last task was now completely healed.

"What are you doing you crazy woman?" he asked, trying to shift out of my grasp.

"Your shoulder. It's healed," I said incredulously.

I ran my thumb over the skin where his scar should have been. But there wasn't so much as a mark there anymore.

"Would you stop that," he complained, pulling away from me and straightening the neck of his black shirt once more.

"Why is it that *you* heal but I don't? We both reset at

the beginning of each cycle, right?" I asked.

"I'm actually surprised you aren't healing. I thought you would just as quickly as me," he said, looking concerned. "Does your head still hurt?"

I nodded but didn't say anything because Hayden was, yet again, running his fingers through my hair to find the bump on my head. Not for the first time, our close proximity and the feeling of his fingers moving over my scalp made me wish he was a nice guy who was sweet and charming, rather than the horror he really was.

"It's getting a little better," he said quietly.

He had my face practically resting on his shoulder as he examined my head and I resisted the urge to actually lay my head there.

"It feels a little better," I agreed, my eyes closed and a daydream in my mind of a sweet Hayden.

Really, my afterlife would be kind of exciting if the company was a bit better. Sure Hayden was nice to look at but being constantly berated by him was not quite pleasant, and it was kind of starting to feel like dangling a caramel apple in front of me that just happened to be rotten in the middle. It looked good but I knew it would make me sick.

"It's not snow time already is it?" Hayden asked, pulling away from me and looking around.

Apparently I'd sounded dazed and confused by our closeness. That was a bit embarrassing.

"So you don't remember what you do when the cycle ends?" I asked, wanting to focus on something other than my conflicted feelings about my Guide.

"I already told you, I know I'm doing something between these tasks but it's all kind of a blur. When the snow falls, I go to leave and the next thing I know, I'm here at the start of a cycle, waiting for you."

"Hayden," I began seriously as he took a step back so that we could have this conversation without him practically straddling me. "Do you really know what's going on here?"

"Yes, Isla. Everything's fine," he said in exasperation.

"No, I mean it. Do you know what's going to happen to me when I reach my Destination?"

Hayden thought about this for a moment. I was sure I already knew the answer, but I wanted to hear from him that we were all pretty much in the dark about what was going on. Since the last task, I'd begun to worry that maybe reaching my Destination wasn't such a good thing. If Hayden didn't even know what was in store for me, who was to say it was a good place I'd be going to?

"I feel like I must have known at some point," Hayden

said, looking angry that he couldn't remember the most basic motivation for him as a Guide. "And I feel like I know when I'm not with you. But once the cycle restarts and I come to guide you I can't remember."

"That's not exactly encouraging," I told him.

"I don't know how many times I can repeat this to you, but I know it's going to be fine… *if* you reach your Destination. I can't give you a reason, but I know it's bad to fail these tasks and it's good for you to get to your Destination, and for now that's going to have to be good enough for you."

It wasn't good enough for me but I didn't think saying that to Hayden would really help anything, so I kept my mouth shut. I was already putting my life (or my second life) in the hands of this complete maniac, but now I just had to trust that I was doing it for a good reason. We were the blind leading the blind.

Hayden must have sensed my trepidation because instead of making fun of me, he came and sat next to me on the hospital bed. Not quite supportive but not mean either.

"Thank you for saving my life today," I told him again, this time actually meeting his eyes.

"I need to get the merchandise to its Destination safely," he said simply, his eyes holding significant meaning that he wanted me to understand. He was *not* doing this because he cared about me. "I'm nothing more than a deliveryman."

"Understood," I answered, giving him a little salute and trying not to look too offended.

We were both silent for a while; me swinging my dangling feet, and Hayden silently brooding.

"This task today reminded me of my brother Tuck," I said after a long time.

I was unable to handle the silence anymore and wondered why the snow seemed to be taking longer and longer to show up lately. All that did was give me more time to make small talk with a man who was not a fan of small talk.

"You used to go to the junkyard with him all the time when you were younger because he fancied himself an inventor," Hayden said in a monotone voice.

"If you're going to say it like that why don't you just let me tell the story?" I asked in annoyance.

He had a knack for making my memories seem so mundane, no matter how brilliant they were in my mind. If he had access to my memories, why couldn't he feel how special they were to me? Or maybe he could and that was why he tried to belittle them… because he was a mean person.

"Anyway," I said, looking over at Hayden pointedly and silently daring him to interrupt me again. He raised his hands in surrender and beckoned for me to continue. "Tuck thought he was an inventor because he'd seen some infomercial about submitting inventions to this company, so he'd always drag me to the junkyard with him while he built little things out of the scraps."

"It sounds like you had a magical childhood," Hayden said sarcastically.

I guess playing around in a junkyard didn't really seem like a dream come true for a kid, and even though we'd grown up without a lot of the things other kids had, I'd never once felt poor. It didn't matter that Hayden pitied my childhood or whatever he wanted to call the disdain he had for me. I enjoyed every second of my life.

Until that last second right before my brand new truck smashed into a tree.

That second wasn't so great.

"You know Tuck saved my life once?" I asked.

"I didn't," Hayden said, sounding a little surprised.

"Very funny," I countered.

"No, I'm not joking," he said, sounding even more puzzled than before. "Why don't I know that?"

I wasn't sure why he couldn't recall a memory that was, perhaps, one of my most important ones, but it was fun watching him lose a little power over me.

"Since my memories are so mundane I guess I won't tell you," I teased.

"You're just making this up, right?" he asked, still troubled.

"Of course I'm not," I answered with a laugh.

Oh yeah, I was enjoying this way too much. I was sure I should be more concerned about the fact that Hayden mysteriously couldn't recall one of my memories, but the fun outweighed my concern.

By a lot.

"Tuck and I went down to the river one day during the summer. It was incredibly hot and humid out and we couldn't afford to go to the public pool. Tuck felt really bad that I was so miserable so he promised me we'd find some way to go swimming," I began, relenting and just telling Hayden the story.

It was nice to actually have a story to tell him that he didn't already know. Suddenly I was excited to relive this experience.

"We went down to the river, which was pretty disgusting by the way. The water was kind of dirty, but it was cold so we didn't really care. I think at first we were just planning to put our feet in since we were wearing clothes and not bathing suits, but eventually we ended up just splashing and swimming around, not caring that we were getting our clothes soaking wet."

"Swimming in rivers and playing in junkyards. If you're trying to convince me that you aren't an unrefined hick, you aren't doing a very good job," Hayden joked.

I rolled my eyes at his statement.

"So," I said loudly to drown out anything else Hayden might say. "Tuck was swimming in the river and I got it into my head that it would be a good idea to jump off of a tree into the water. Just like the diving board at the public pool."

"Of course you did."

"Tuck kept begging me not to jump, telling me it was too shallow. He even got out of the water and started climbing the tree to get me down, but I got scared that he was really coming up to push me in so I jumped," I said, remembering the sensation of falling through the humid heat then suddenly being engulfed by icy water.

"The current was really strong and I was a little disoriented from the jump, so I couldn't remember which way was up. I actually ended up hitting my head on a rock and then the world went really fuzzy and dark. For a while I thought my shirt was covering my face in the water because I couldn't see and my skin felt like it had all fallen asleep. I remember telling myself over and over not to breathe, no matter how much I wanted to.

"I kept trying to bring my hands up to feel my cheeks because the feeling seemed to be gone from them but I couldn't move my body at all. After a while, I couldn't feel the water around me and I knew I was on dry land, but I still didn't want to breathe."

I paused for a moment, realizing for the first time how similar this memory was to one I had just created a few days before.

"I had the strangest dream while I was passed out. I was sitting in the tree branches above Tuck, and I could see him trying to bring me back to life. My face was muddy and there was blood all around me from where I'd hit my head on the rock. I kept thinking I couldn't go back and I couldn't take a breath, but suddenly I wanted nothing more than to tell Tuck I was okay. The desire to see him again was so overwhelming that I forced myself to take a breath."

I stopped speaking. My eyes were burning at the thought that my latest story had ended quite differently from this one.

"And?" Hayden asked, sounding more interested than I'd ever heard him, which was good. I couldn't bear to have him belittle this memory that I held so dear.

"And I woke up," I said simply. "Tuck was kneeling over me. Praying I think. And he looked white as a ghost. I got ten stitches at the nape of my neck and grounded for a week for swimming in the river when Mama and Daddy had told us not to. I still have a scar."

I gathered my hair up and turned my back to Hayden to show him the now small scar just below my hairline on the nape of my neck.

He traced it with his finger for a moment, not making any comment on my story. Though I guess he wasn't making fun of me either so that was something.

"Tuck was always the stereotypical protective big brother. He was always there to keep me safe," I said, my voice catching unexpectedly as I faced Hayden again.

"He's still alive," Hayden pointed out, obviously misinterpreting my sadness.

"But he couldn't save me this time," I explained.

"Yeah, but it wasn't his fault that you died."

He still wasn't understanding me.

"It doesn't matter," I said, my voice shaking as tears began to slide over my cheeks. "He'll blame himself for not being able to help me. That's just how he is. He feels like it's his job to keep everyone safe. He works nonstop to contribute to the family. He never took his football scholarship because he was worried that if he left, Mama and Daddy wouldn't be able to make it on their income alone.

"He's selfless."

I wiped the few stray tears away from my cheeks, not wanting to think about Tuck anymore. Or how I'd never see my family again.

Hayden didn't respond to my story, but he very slowly moved his hand over on the bed so that it rested on top of mine. As small as the gesture was, I knew it was a big deal for Hayden to show any sort of support, and I appreciated it immensely.

"You know, every time you talk about dying, you talk about how it's affected everyone but you. Why is that?" he asked after a moment.

"I don't know," I lied.

"Are you really that unconcerned with your own ambitions and feelings that you just don't care about the fact that your life was cut off so abruptly?"

"Of course I care," I answered. "You'd have to be crazy to not be at least a little upset that all of the things you wanted to do have been stolen away from you."

"I wasn't going to put 'crazy' past you. I just wanted to make sure."

"Shut up," I said playfully, laughing for a moment before it was cut off by a post-cry hiccup, which only made me laugh more.

I used the hand that Hayden wasn't sort of holding to wipe the last of my tears away.

"There were a lot of things I wanted to do," I assured him. "Monica and I wanted to travel overseas."

I left out the fact that we were hoping to meet some cute boys with English accents, since that would probably clue him into the fact that, despite how mean he was, I was a sucker for a good English accent.

"There was this boy who worked at the bookstore that I always wanted to ask out, but never did. Actually I'd made a pact with Monica that I'd give him my number the day after we graduated. Which would have been the day after I died," I said in slight amusement. "I hope she went on a date with him to honor my memory."

"You are one of a kind, Isla Edison," Hayden told me.

"How do you know my last name?" I asked him.

"How can I perfectly recall all but one of your memories?" he asked rhetorically.

“Good point,” I agreed before going back on to my rambling thoughts. “Anyway, I could tell Monica liked that boy too, so I hope she doesn’t refrain from talking to him because she’s scared I’m going to haunt her or something. Speaking of which! After these tasks are all done, can I go back to visit my family as a ghost or something?”

Hayden laughed at this question. I’d take that as a “no”.

“First off, ghosts aren’t real. And second, all I know is how to get you to your Destination. Anything else, you’re going to have to take up with whoever is on the other side for you.”

“Will you not come with me?” I asked, suddenly feeling a little sad at the idea of not having Hayden around, no matter how unpleasant he was.

“Of course I can’t come with you,” he stated.

I couldn’t tell how he felt about the situation when he simply defaulted to his normal unhappy setting, but I liked to think that Hayden was slowly coming to think of me as a friend. He was sort of turning into my unwilling hostage and I had every intention of forcing him to be happier whether he liked it or not.

Curious to know if he thought of me as a friend now, I opened my mouth to ask him, but quickly shut it again when the snow started to fall. I definitely didn't want to ask a question like that when Hayden had such a perfect excuse to leave abruptly without answering.

I could feel my eyelids growing heavy. Hayden took his hand off of mine and suddenly he was cradling my head as he lowered me into a laying position on the bed. He was actually kind of helping me.

I fought to keep my eyes open or even to say something to him about how nice it was to have him being sweet to me, but I couldn't seem to form the sentence. The desire to sleep was just too much.

Just as my eyes closed completely, I felt Hayden tuck a stray hair behind my ear, his hand brushing against my cheek for just a moment longer than it needed to and I knew the answer to my question without ever having to ask it.

Hayden was my unwilling friend.

CHAPTER 16

"Isla?"

The word was so faint that I hardly expelled the effort to open my eyes at the sound. My body still felt heavy from the snow yesterday and my head was hurting where the bump refused to go away.

"Isla?"

The word came again. Only this time I actually sat bolt upright. It wasn't the fact that my name was being called; it was the voice calling it.

"Daddy?" I whispered to the still empty office.

Paper crackled underneath me as I pivoted on the hospital bed and let my bare feet touch the cold linoleum floor.

I hadn't taken my boots off the night before when I'd fallen asleep. The only thing I could think was that maybe Hayden had removed them for me while I was sleeping.

Somehow, that didn't really match up with the normal image of my Guide. I couldn't see him as the sweet doting type.

Sun was still streaming in lazy beams through the shades in the office and I had to think this was very early in the cycle for the sun to still be out. I wouldn't be surprised if Hayden wasn't even here yet. He only seemed to show up once the sun melted away, allowing itself to be subdued by the ever-present fog.

"Daddy?" I called again, this time standing from the bed and searching the small room.

I didn't really need to walk to search, since the room was so incredibly tiny. Still, I didn't want to run the risk that by some miracle my father might be here and I wouldn't get the chance to see him.

Maybe this was what happened once you got closer to your Destination. Maybe they let you see a member of your family to give you some encouragement or moral support.

The sun was already starting to fade and soon the fog darkened the room considerably, leaving only the flickering fluorescent light above my head.

It didn't take long for me to confirm that my dad, in fact, wasn't in the room. It didn't really come as a surprise to me but I'd still had a hope, in the back of my mind, that

I'd be able to see him one last time.

Feeling like I shouldn't dwell on my moment of hallucination for too long, I put my boots on and made my way outside, assuming I'd run into my Guide there and he'd either be able to explain what had happened, or give me another impossible task to take my mind off of my own loneliness.

"Bout time you showed up," Hayden called to me, as if on cue.

He was standing on top of a grassy hill, looking down at me in exasperation. Apparently I was able to annoy him before I'd even opened my mouth.

"Hayden, I need to ask you something," I said as I jogged over to him.

I would have asked him about the voice I'd heard only moments before. I had every intention of asking him if it was possible that my dad might be here. But instead my words were cut short when I saw the brightly colored puddles that dotted the land in front of me.

"Yellowstone?" I guessed, trying to make sense of the green valley surrounding the rocky, neon colored pools.

"Sort of," Hayden confirmed, sounding only mildly impressed by my guess. "Yellowstone with a few alterations."

"At least it's not a junk yard, right?" I asked, trying to joke but getting no response from my Guide. "Hey there's a place in Yellowstone called Hayden Valley… so that's… interesting," I finished lamely.

He wasn't in the mood for jokes today. I was guessing it was because he'd used up all of his nice energy last night when he helped me into bed.

But really, if I was making everything in these cycles up, maybe I'd made Hayden up. And maybe my perfect man was a dark and mysterious British man who was named after a place in Yellowstone. It actually made a lot of sense.

"As long as I don't have to fight off bears or stop an unstoppable geyser I think I can handle this."

"You don't even know what the task is yet," Hayden pointed out.

He sounded bored.

"I know it's not a giant robot spider that wants to cut me in half, or a flesh-eating zombie who's after my brains. So that's a step up."

"What was your question?" he asked, obviously wanting to change the subject away from whatever aspect of my personality was bugging him at the moment.

I considered how I could phrase my question for a

moment. I couldn't just ask if my dad was here because Hayden would say I was being homesick and weak. On the other hand, I couldn't say I'd heard his voice because then he'd be sure I was completely nuts.

"I wanted to know how many tasks there are," I finally said. And while that wasn't actually the question I had intended to ask him, it was something I had been wondering about for some time.

"I can't believe it took you this long to ask me that," he said condescendingly before I gave him a look that said I was having none of his attitude today.

"There are only six tasks," he amended.

"Six?" I repeated. "So after this I only have one more?"

It didn't seem possible that I was actually this close to being done with the crazy and seemingly random tasks. This newfound knowledge meant that I'd actually need to think about if I wanted to go to my Destination or not. After all, even Hayden couldn't tell me what it actually meant to reach my Destination.

For all he knew, it could mean I was volunteering to become a Guide myself. Or maybe I'd simply pass through the door and that would be the end of me. I'd be cast into an eternity of nothingness.

"Are you just going to stand there, or is it all right with you if we get on with things?" he asked, and had I not been so deep in thought I would have shot him another look. Instead I simply nodded distractedly. "Fantastic."

Hayden began walking down the hill towards the pools of water though I didn't follow behind him. Suddenly, with the end so close, I wasn't sure how I felt about rushing through each task in the hopes that I'd get to my unknown Destination sooner.

Why was I so anxious to get to this place if I didn't even know if it would be an improvement on my current situation?

"I know it's a bit early, but as a general rule you need to be present to complete these tasks," Hayden called over his shoulder, stopping his trek down the hill and turning to give me an appraising look. "I don't want to overwhelm you with that fact or anything."

He was looking at me expectantly, waiting for me to make a snarky remark right back at him or whine about how mean he always was to me. It was his joy in life to do this little back-and-forth exchange and be as terrible as he possibly could be. But suddenly, I wanted nothing more than time that I didn't have. I didn't want to be forced to begin the task and I couldn't care less if that messed up

Hayden's quota somehow.

Instead of answering him, I turned around and began walking towards the wooded area away from both the safe house and the task ahead.

"Isla?" Hayden asked, sounding confused at first, and I could only wonder how long it would take for his confusion to be replaced by anger.

His anger wasn't usually too far from the surface to begin with.

Ignoring his calls, I stopped under the shade of the tall pine trees and sat on the ground, giving no mind to the dirt I'd inevitably get on my skirt. In the long run it didn't matter since A) I was dead, and B) my dress would simply clean itself the next morning.

"What do you think you're doing?" Hayden asked, his previously subdued anger now showing through the vein on his forehead.

"I'm sitting," I replied with a too-sweet smile.

"Yeah, I can see that. I'm not an idiot but maybe I need to rephrase the question so that *you'll* understand. Why aren't you doing the task?"

I refrained from rolling my eyes at his less-than-friendly tone.

"Why should I be so anxious to get to my

Destination?"

"Oh please not this again," he said in complete and utter exasperation. "I swear pairing me with you is some kind of punishment."

"I'm serious, Hayden!"

"So am I."

"If you don't even know what my Destination is, then why should I want to go there?" I asked. "It might end up being something bad."

"It's called having a little faith," he said, not making any move to sit down next to me, but not screaming and throwing things at me either. "You just have to trust me."

"Trust you?" I laughed. "I trust you about as far as I can spit."

"Charming expression."

"Why on earth would I trust you? You've given me absolutely no reason to."

"You've made it this far haven't you?" he asked smugly.

"No thanks to you. I've made it this far despite your best efforts to sabotage me at every turn."

"So we're just forgetting about the help I've given you?" he asked, surprising me that he was actually the one to bring up the one time he'd broken the rules for me.

"Sorry. Thanks for the one time you helped me because I was about to be sliced in half and you exercised one ounce of human decency," I amended sarcastically.

Really, I was grateful that he'd helped me during the last task since I was definitely only a few seconds from dying again. But still, it seemed like the only decent thing to do to break the rules a bit to stop someone from being torn to pieces. I would hope Hayden had at least *that* much humanity in him.

"What are you talking about? You needed motivation for the first task and I provide that to ensure you didn't fail," he said, sounding like he really believed his own terrible reasoning. "You didn't think you could jump over the gap on the second task so I helped you along."

He failed to mention that "helping me along" meant lying to me and practically throwing me over the ledge against my will.

"I stayed conscious long enough to explain what the third task was so that you'd have an idea of what you were supposed to do. Not to mention the fact that I had to endure your terrible hospitality and having an arrow shot through my shoulder."

When he said everything back-to-back like that, I could almost understand his unsound logic. But then I'd remember how he'd discouraged me, lied to me, taunted me, and generally made me miserable.

"You really think you've been helping me?" I asked in disbelief.

"You really think I haven't been?" he asked, equally shocked by my view.

"You're a real piece of work, you know that?"

Shaking my head I got to my feet, brushed off my dress, and began walking back in the direction of the task. I knew Hayden wouldn't let me waiver from our strict self-imposed itinerary for long, but I'd hoped he would give me at least a few minutes to think things through.

"Arrogant, self-important, conceited man," I mumbled under my breath, while Hayden walked by my side with a self-satisfied smile on his handsome face.

He was enjoying my anger way too much.

"You might want to stop for a second so I can tell you about the task," he began, though I completely ignored him and continued walking towards the brightly colored pools in front of me.

"I'm sure you have lots of 'helpful' things to tell me," I shot back sarcastically, fuming at just how crazy Hayden made me.

I didn't slow my pace at all, practically jogging down

the hill until I was right in front of the rocky landscape.

“Hey!” Hayden shouted, grabbing me by my upper arm and pulling me backwards into his chest with a bit too much force.

“What?” I yelled back, spinning around to face him.

My intimidation factor was somewhat lessened by our height difference. Staring up at someone angrily while resisting the urge to stand on your tip toes wasn’t exactly terrifying. It was just a little sad.

His face quickly transitioned from urgently annoyed to cool and cocky once more.

“As much as you don’t like me, you’re going to need to listen to my instructions for this next one,” Hayden said disinterestedly.

He always sounded so detached and above it all. It was infuriating.

“What’s the task,” I asked, turning away from him.

I tried to make my voice sound as annoyed as I possibly could, though I suspected the message still didn’t quite get through to him.

“Task five: Strategy.”

“Strategy. I can do strategy,” I said. “Strategy usually doesn’t involved being chased, or killed, or eaten.”

“Not *usually*,” Hayden began with a gleeful

expression.

"Seriously?" I asked. "What's going to kill me this time?"

"A pool of acid," he responded simply.

I took a few steps away from the brightly colored puddle in front of me and finally took a good look around. The terrain in front of me was rocky and desert like, despite the woods around this little valley. I could see the safe house in the distance at the top of a series of podium like structures made from rock.

It looked like after navigating the valley full of pools, I'd need to jump from podium to podium until I got to the safe house, which resided on the tallest of the rocks.

"So the pools are acid?" I asked with a humorless laugh.

"This is why I need to explain it to you… to *help* you like I always do," he said.

I thought his use of the word "help" was a bit loose, but didn't say anything. I let my pride take a back seat for a moment so that I wouldn't end up falling into a pool of acid. A fair trade off.

"First of all, you'll need these," he said, handing me five small glass vials, each with a different colored liquid inside. "Each liquid does something different depending on the color. Now it doesn't matter if you drink it or simply touch it with your skin, the effect will still work."

Glancing out over the pools once more, things were beginning to make sense.

"Not all of the pools are acid," I guessed.

"Only the orange ones," he confirmed.

"And I luckily don't have an orange vial."

"I resisted the temptation."

"How very 'helpful' of you Hayden," I said, making sure I emphasized the word he didn't seem to understand.

"I'm nothing if not helpful."

"I would never call you 'nothing'," I responded sweetly.

He shot me a fake and short lived smile before continuing.

"I'm only going to say this once, so I suggest you make a mental note of which colors do what," he went on. "When you leave the grass you won't have control over your own body anymore. You'll begin walking and there's no way to stop yourself until the task is complete. That's very important to understand."

"Got it," I said with a wave of my hand.

"Once you start this task, you cannot stop it," he emphasized, obviously not trusting that I really understood him.

"Oh. Kay," I said dramatically, matching his serious tone, though mine was completely sarcastic.

"You'll use the liquid in the vials and the different pools to navigate yourself through the landscape. In fact, you should probably take your boots off so you can ensure the liquid touches your skin if you walk through it."

I gave him an odd look but followed his directions, taking my boots off and handing them over to him once more.

"The first two colors are pretty easy. The red liquid slows you down and the green liquid speeds you up. Just like traffic lights."

"That's simple enough so far."

"The blue liquid will allow you to go backwards but only for a few seconds before you'll automatically start moving forward again. But there's no liquid that will change your backward movement. You just have to wait until the blue wears off if you want to move forward. The purple liquid will help you jump over gaps and obstacles, including pools, which might just save your life if that pool happens to be orange."

"Which would make it acid," I repeated, just to show that I was being a good little listener.

“Very good.”

“So what does the yellow vial do?” I asked.

“Turns the sun back on,” he explained, completely baffling me.

“Wait. What?”

“Every once in a while, the sun is going to go out on you. When that happens you’ll need to drink from the yellow vial to ignite it again. On that note, you may want to conserve that one if you can.”

“Somehow I missed the whole ‘sun going out’ thing on my trip to Yellowstone when I was little,” I deadpanned.

“Not sure how you could have,” Hayden responded.

“Must be because I’m an uneducated hick.”

“I was going to say it’s because you’re a woman. But it’s probably a combination of the two,” he agreed with a solemn nod.

I reached out to hit his arm but ended up dropping the yellow vial in the process. It shattered the second it hit the rocky ground and I gasped, bringing my hand up to my mouth in shock.

“Would you please at least begin the task before completely failing it?” Hayden asked with a raise of his eyebrow as he pulled another yellow vial from his pants pocket and handed it to me.

"Sorry," I responded with a wince.

"I'll forgive you this once. Now I'm sure it's pretty obvious by this point, but your goal is to get to the safe house up there and avoid falling into the acid."

"And the strategy comes in where?"

"You can only use one color at a time. Not only that, but you have a limited amount of each liquid so make sure you don't use up all of the yellow in your vial if there's a perfectly good yellow pool right in front of you. In fact, I'd avoid using the vials at all unless you absolutely have to. The pools are a much better option."

"Got it. Is there anything else?"

"Just one thing," Hayden said, looking like he had absolutely no faith in me. "Good luck."

CHAPTER 17

"This isn't so bad," I called over to Hayden; and so far, it wasn't.

Of course I hadn't run into any pools of acid yet and I hadn't really needed to use the vials.

"Would you stop talking and just focus please?" he asked.

Hayden had been walking along the perimeter of the task, avoiding the pools and not offering any help. It seemed like he was hardly paying attention to me at all, though it was surprising that he was staying with me rather than meeting me at the safe house like he normally did.

I considered how close we were to reaching my Destination and I couldn't help but think that made him nervous. This was the closest he'd gotten to successfully guiding someone and now he was taking extra precautions, as was evident by his refusal to leave while I completed the task.

"There's a purple pool coming up which is…," I let my words trail off as I racked my memory. Good thing I wasn't in any danger yet since I seemed to forget what each color did almost instantly. "Jumping?" I guessed.

Hayden looked extremely put out by the cavalier manner in which I was treating this task, but his anxiety made me happy.

My legs continued to carry my forward of their own accord.

At first when I'd begun the task, the loss of control over my own legs had frightened me. Now, I wished I could turn this ability on whenever I wanted. It was like driving a car; I got to my destination but I didn't have to expel any energy to do it.

The second my bare foot touched the purple puddle in front of me I felt my knees bend and my legs flex. In the next instant, I was being propelled through the air at an alarming rate; the wind whistling past my ears and my hair fanning out around me as I reached the peak of my arc.

The jump didn't move me forward as much as I'd hoped. Instead it seemed to be a very vertical jump, and by the time my feet hit the ground once more, I had barely cleared the purple pool.

“Good to know my ‘jumping’ is so wimpy,” I said to Hayden, hoping I’d be able to clear the gaps between each podium on the way to the safe house.

“Think of the other colors,” he responded cryptically.

I knew he couldn’t help me outright, but it sure seemed like he wanted to. I didn’t think Hayden trusted me to complete this task at all.

“I can’t use two at a time,” I answered in confusion.

“True, but some of the effects last for at least a few seconds.”

I looked down at the vials in my hands and suddenly wondered how long the green liquid would speed me up. Really, if it were any duration of time longer than a few seconds I’d have time to try some of the purple liquid and get a running jump as a result.

“Looks like you’ll have an opportunity to test it out up here,” Hayden told me and sure enough, a green pool sat only a few feet ahead of me.

The next pool, only a few more yards away, was orange.

“Acid,” I said to myself, noting that I should have a purple vial ready for when I reached the deadly pool.

With no way to stop it, my feet touched the green-colored puddle and I instantly began running at a breakneck speed; faster than I ever would have been able to sprint on my own. I held the purple vial to my lips for just a moment, waiting until the very last second to take a sip.

Surprisingly, the liquid tasted just how it looked; like a melted grape popsicle. To say I was pleasantly surprised would be an understatement. I'd figured that in this place where everything seemed like it was out to get me, the liquid in each vial would taste like rotten eggs.

In a split second, my body was forced to jump and I was propelled over the orange pool as well as a yellow pool. Once my feet hit the ground again I continued to run for a good thirty seconds before slowing my pace once more.

"Wow," I breathed.

I was surprised I had actually managed to clear the pool, and was exhilarated by the feeling of flying I had just experienced.

"Guess it lasts for quite a while," I called over to Hayden.

"You dropped the red vial," he responded, his hand over his face as if he couldn't bear to look at me and all of my failures.

"Uh oh," I said, looking behind me at the smashed red vial.

I had dropped it behind the yellow pool and suddenly, I couldn't remember which vial would take me backwards.

"I didn't really need to slow down anyway, I've got this," I told Hayden, sounding even less confident than I felt. "Besides, all of these vials are just weighing me down and confusing me."

With that, I dropped the blue vial on the ground, remembering finally which color would take me backwards after deciding it wasn't important.

"What are you doing?" Hayden practically shouted. "Are you completely insane?"

"I don't need to go backwards. Why on earth would I need that?" I asked, looking at the other colors in my hands and wondering which ones I could discard just as the sun went out.

"Crap," I mumbled.

I hadn't been looking ahead so I couldn't be sure there wasn't an acid pool only a few steps away. Bringing each vial to my nose in turn, I hoped the rest would smell how they looked and give me some indication of what they were, since it was far too dark to see what colors the containers held.

The first smelled like grape and I knew it was the jumping vial. Definitely didn't need that at the moment.

The next vial smelled like apples and for a moment I wondered how I could possibly still be holding the red liquid when I'd seen it smashed behind me.

"Green apples," I clarified after a moment, leaving only one other color in my hand.

The lemony liquid hit my tongue with a vengeance, instantly igniting the sun once more and alerting me to the orange pool only a few steps ahead. Moving quickly I took a small sip of the green, followed almost immediately by the purple, giving me enough of a running jump to get past the final pool of acid before the podium jumping that lay ahead.

"Well done," Hayden said, though I couldn't tell if he was being sarcastic or not.

It was always safer to assume he was defaulting into his normal habits.

"Now I just have to impossibly jump from podium to podium," I responded.

Looking at the task ahead I tried to assess the whole thing like one of the video games my brother had always forced me to play with him in the arcade. The green liquid definitely lasted long enough to keep me running all the way to the safe house. Technically, I could drink the rest of the green liquid, throw it out, and only have to worry about the purple and yellow.

It would definitely simplify things to only have two vials to worry about.

"You look like you're thinking, and that always worries me," Hayden called.

"Just thinking of ways to get rid of even more vials," I assured him, though he looked far from assured.

"You do realize what a stupid idea it is to get rid of vials as you go, right? There's a reason you need each of those, and getting rid of them isn't going to do you any favors."

"I'm fine," I replied, not listening to his advice for a second. "Here we go!"

With that, I drank the rest of the green vial and threw it to the ground, loosely holding the yellow vial in my hand while the purple one was brought to my lips, ready for every gap that came my way.

I could only guess at what was on the ground between each podium, but if I was being logical, I'd say an orange pool of acid was the most likely option. Not a theory I really wanted to test out.

My legs carried me forward quickly, over the rocky terrain and up the steep slope towards the first podium. As soon as I neared the first gap, I drank a bit of the purple liquid, causing me to jump through the air and land gracefully on the second podium.

I repeated this pattern three times until I was on the last stretch of elevated land, just before safe house on the other side of my last gap.

“Piece of cake,” I called to Hayden who now stood at the front door of the safe house.

“You’re a bit of a show off. Did you know that?”

“It’s not showing off if it’s pure skill,” I joked.

“Yeah it is.”

I grinned over at him happily, finding that this task was actually exciting rather than horrifying and it had lightened my mood considerably.

I still ran at full speed, though I could swear I was slowing down every second. As long as I had enough speed to bridge the last gap, I didn’t care.

“Maybe you should stop gloating and pay attention so you time the jump properly,” Hayden suggested.

“Yeah, I’ll get right on that,” I shot back with a laugh just as the sun went out, casting me into complete darkness.

My feet continued to run and the final gap continued to loom ever closer, but suddenly, in my moment of panic I couldn’t remember which vial held the purple liquid.

“I need to turn the sun back on!” I shouted. “Also, I

never thought I'd utter that sentence."

"Isla, you're getting really close to the edge. I suggest you figure it out quickly," Hayden called, sounding surprisingly panicked.

I wasn't sure how he could see that I was getting close to the edge in the pitch blackness, but I assumed it was some sort of perk for being a Guide.

I could sense my time running out as I continued on my full out sprint towards the ledge and all I could think was, "Left hand or right hand? Which one is purple?"

"Isla!" Hayden called again, this time, sounding only two seconds away from really letting me have it.

I must have been getting close to the ledge.

"I don't remember if the purple vial is in my right or left hand," I yelled back, now completely frantic.

I brought both vials up to my nose, trying to distinguish between the two scents but knew I was almost out of time.

"It's in your left hand!" Hayden screamed at me.

Without questioning him, I quickly drank the liquid in my left hand and felt my feet leave the ground for a breathtaking moment. Both vials dropped from my grasp and I hoped I wouldn't need them any longer once I made it to the safe house.

My feet hit the soft grass of the final podium and I immediately barreled right into a solid figure, sending us both sprawling onto the ground. The sun ignited itself once more and I looked up at Hayden who, for the second time since meeting him, I was laying on top of. Our chins were touching and despite the confusing feelings that were suddenly coming to life within me, I simply breathed out a huge sigh of relief.

"Thanks," I whispered to him.

"Don't mention it," he returned, equally as breathless.

For someone who was so bent on following the rules, it didn't escape my notice just how many times Hayden had willingly broken them for me.

CHAPTER 18

There was something wrong with the safe house. Almost everything was identical to the rooms I had stayed in before this one, but one thing was missing that I couldn't quite explain: Hayden's rocking chair.

I didn't bring this fact to his attention, though I knew he was aware of it. My imagination had created each task and each safe house, and up until this point, I had always created a space for myself, and a space for my Guide. But for some unknown reason, today my mind hadn't given Hayden his own space and I didn't know if it was because somewhere deep inside of me I wanted him out of the safe house, or if, by some miracle, I wanted him to be forced to sit beside me.

Either way, we both soon found ourselves sitting side by side on the wooden bed of the cabin-like safe house, staring at the crackling fire and not saying a word.

Hayden's knee rested against mine and it felt like there was an electric charge between us, though looking over at my Guide, he looked as if he could care less where he sat. He continued to stare at the fire, looking dark and misguided and just generally unpleasant.

It was a safe bet that he wasn't feeling whatever electricity I was making up between us.

"Why did you help me? Again?" I asked quietly, looking down at my hands, which I was wringing in my lap.

"I didn't want you to get hurt," he replied.

It was a simple enough answer. Uncomplicated. But the fact that it was Hayden saying he didn't want me to get hurt gave it a whole new meaning. He wasn't exactly the type of person to care about the well-being of others and he took pride in revealing that little detail. It would have been all too easy for him to say he didn't want to fail at getting another dead girl to her Destination, but he hadn't. And suddenly, my brain was in full on over-analyze-everything mode.

"Won't you get in trouble for breaking the rules?"

"The way I figure it, it was a strategy test," he reasoned. "You already figured out the strategy and knew what you wanted to do. Knowing which vial was in which hand wasn't really part of the strategy aspect."

I turned this over in my mind for a moment, wondering if this really was a legitimate way around the rules. It seemed fair enough and if anyone would be aware of the rules it was Hayden. He was a rule follower if nothing else.

"Well either way, I appreciate it," I told him, still not looking over at him.

It was odd how only a few hours ago I'd wanted to kill him. *Most* of the time I wanted to kill him actually. He was completely rude, self-centered, and just plain mean. But the longer he and I had been forced to be together, the more he had let his gruff exterior slip. He kept accidentally showing me that he could be nice deep down.

The funny thing was, he was always at his nicest when he was completely panicked and had to make a split second decision. My daddy had always said you'd truly know a man when he was desperate. That's when he'd let his true colors show.

So was Hayden a nice guy pretending to be mean? Or was he a mean guy who would do the right thing when it came down to the wire?

"Stop doing that, it's annoying," Hayden finally said, acting like his usual self.

"Doing what?"

"Stop thinking so loudly."

"Oh, what? You can hear my thoughts?" I asked skeptically.

I had no doubt Hayden had some sort of power here, but I highly doubted his power spanned that great a distance.

"Of course I can't read your thoughts, but you're wringing your hands and biting your lip. That's what you do right before you say something *you* think is clever."

"But it's not really clever?" I asked, trying not to laugh at just how mad I seemed to make him.

"Not really, no."

"It must be hard for you here, Hayden," I said, my voice dripping with mock sympathy.

"Why?"

"Being forced to be stuck with someone so beneath you."

"Most people are beneath me. You get used to it after a while," he responded and for a moment, I thought he was being serious.

Then he turned and looked at me with a hint of a smile on his face.

"Relax, Isla. I was joking."

"You're not really much of a comedian. You should

stick to what you know."

"Which would be... what? Making you so mad that you try to jump off a cliff?" he asked with a raised eyebrow.

"You are quite amazing at that actually," I conceded.

"And what are you good at? Besides annoying me to no end."

"I'm a good singer," I offered. "And no I won't demonstrate."

"Thank goodness."

I gave him an icy look at his statement but it quickly broke across my face into a smile.

"My parents always made fun of me for majoring in vocal performance. They said I was paying a bunch of money to get a degree in something you didn't need a degree for."

"They were kind of right," Hayden pointed out with a fake wince.

"Maybe. But I got to have the full college experience and I learned the theories behind vocal performance that I wouldn't know otherwise."

"I'm sure that's helped you out a lot," he responded sarcastically.

"Maybe if I hadn't tried to break the windshield with

my forehead it would have worked out well," I joked back, though joking about my death put a bad taste in my mouth so I quickly went on. "My parents were always really supportive though, no matter how much they made fun of me. They were proud that I'd be the first person in our family to graduate from a university."

"What can you even do with a vocal performance degree?" Hayden asked, not sounding very impressed by my artsy major.

"I can be a singer or I can teach voice lessons. There's a lot I can do with it… could do," I amended. "I'd sing at weddings sometimes or at the fair. Once I sang the national anthem at a baseball game. That was fun."

I hadn't exactly had much time to use my degree, but I suddenly felt a sense of loss over the dreams I'd wanted to fulfill that were now out of reach.

"I wrote my own music," I said proudly, looking over at Hayden with a smile and trying to turn this conversation into a happy one, rather than the pity party it was turning into.

"Congratulations?" he asked.

"Hey, that's really hard to do," I exclaimed, hitting him playfully on the shoulder.

My boots were discarded on the wooden floor and I

lifted my feet up onto the bed, tucking them underneath me so that my bare knees rested next to Hayden's hips and I could get a better look at him.

"I have about a dozen songs hidden under my bed. Music and lyrics all done and ready to be recorded," I told Hayden, grinning as I recounted my little secret. "As a graduation present to myself, I was going to rent a recording booth and put all of my songs on a CD to send out to local record labels."

"Okay, you have to tell me honestly," Hayden said, seeming to loosen up a little at my relaxed posture. Before we had both been sitting stiffly at attention. "Were you any good?"

"I don't know how to answer that without sounding conceited, but I was *very* good," I said, laughing a bit at my own description of myself. "There's no way to sound humble saying that, is there?" I asked, crinkling my nose up at him.

"I don't think so, but you put forth a valiant effort. Well done," Hayden replied, now laughing as well.

His laugh was deep and rich. It gave me goose bumps.

"Please tell me you don't sing country music or I'll be forced to kick you out of the safe house this instant."

"What's wrong with country?" I asked, sounding

offended even though I wasn't.

"Everyone in the South fancies themselves a country singer and most of them are awful," he said, giving me a look. "In fact, the entire genre is awful in and of itself so I can't really blame the people who sing it. There's just no saving that music."

"You are the most unpleasant person I've ever met," I told him with a laugh, tucking my hair behind my ear.

"Well I don't sing country, so that's not possible."

I resisted the urge to reach out and hit him again.

"I like country," I said.

"Of course you do. You're a backwoods hick from North Carolina."

"North Carolina isn't even the *South* south," I said defensively.

"It's south enough for you to have that terrible accent," he pointed out, now openly grinning at me.

It was a sight I wasn't used to, and it threw me off momentarily.

"Well you'll be happy to know I don't sing country."

"I think you're lying," he said, narrowing his eyes playfully as if he were trying to read me.

It was almost as if knocking Hayden over today (for the second time) had rewired his brain and he suddenly didn't think it would be the end of the world if he joked around with me or acted like a decent human being. It was a nice change to say the least.

"I swear," I told him, holding up my hand. "Scout's honor."

"Then what do you sing?"

"I sing folk music," I said smugly.

"That's the same thing!" he practically shouted, still grinning.

"No it's not! Folk is more like *Mumford and Sons*. They aren't country."

"That's true," he agreed.

"Plus they have those amazing accents."

"What, English accents? You think an English accent is nice?" he asked, sounding like that was the most ridiculous thing he'd ever heard.

I guessed the look he was giving me was very similar to the look I gave people when they said they liked Southern accents. To me, I didn't even have an accent so how could it be special or different?

"Not that I would ever want to admit this to *you*, but I happen to have a soft spot for English accents," I said, slightly embarrassed to reveal this detail to Hayden.

He looked slightly skeptical of this revelation, but

leaned in closer to me, as if testing the theory. This was definitely not the Hayden I was used to. Normally he was doing anything he could to get away from me. Close proximity was *not* his thing.

"A soft spot huh?" he asked quietly, still coming ever closer to me. "So do you think my accent is charming then?"

Our blue eyes were locked on each other as he stopped his forward progression, so close to me that I could smell the clean scent of soap on him. His face was out of focus at this proximity but I could see a distant look in his eyes, as if he were drowsy. Or maybe it was just content? I couldn't tell, but I did know it wasn't a look I'd seen him wear before.

"When you aren't saying terrible things it is," I whispered, scared to death that I was misreading the signals he was sending me. "But you're almost always saying terrible things."

My heart was pounding so hard that my hands shook, but miraculously, I didn't have a million thoughts running through my mind like I should have. I only wondered if Hayden could possibly be getting ready to kiss me or if he was going to suddenly pull away and laugh at me for thinking he'd ever want to kiss me.

His nose was touching mine now and his blue eyes were drifting lazily over my face and all I could think was, “This is the longest build up ever”. I had to admit though, the lead up to a first kiss was usually the best part, so I let myself enjoy it, without considering the humiliating possibility that it wouldn’t happen.

“I’m sorry about that, Isla,” he finally whispered back to me, the space between us proving to be too much for him as he closed the distance and eliminated the gap.

I tilted my head back and closed my eyes, as his hands tentatively cupped my cheeks, resting gently beneath my jaw bone. I wasn’t sure what I should do with my shaking hands at this odd angle so I turned my body towards him, letting my fingers slide over his broad shoulders and link together behind his neck.

Despite the light touch in his hands, the kiss was deep and perfect. It was more real than the falling sensation I’d experience only days before when this very same man had pushed me off a cliff.

We definitely had a dysfunctional relationship.

After a while I could feel Hayden’s lips curl up into a smile beneath mine, and I could sense that he wanted to say something but I didn’t let him. I leaned in to him even more, determined to enjoy every single moment of this too perfect kiss. His hands left my cheeks and travelled down my arms, coming to rest on my waist where the pressure of his fingertips sent goose bumps over my skin.

It was almost painful how amazingly perfect the kiss felt.

Until I felt a snowflake hit my cheek and my mind instantly went fuzzy.

I stopped kissing Hayden but kept my lips against his lightly, just barely touching.

"Your mind has terrible timing," Hayden said, tickling my lips with his speech and giving me one last kiss as I struggled to keep myself upright.

"I don't want you to go," I said sleepily, not sure if my words were making any sense as he gently lowered me onto the bed.

"I honestly never thought I'd say this to you, but I don't want to go either," he admitted.

And with that, he brushed his lips over my forehead and I fell into a forced sleep with the most peaceful smile I'd ever worn on my still tingling lips.

CHAPTER 19

When I woke the next morning, my head ached and the small amount of light coming in through the closed shutters was all too bright. I draped my arm over my eyes and pulled the quilt up to my chin, not really feeling like getting out of bed for my final cycle.

I was lucky my sleep each night was forced or I was sure I wouldn't have gotten any rest with the thought of my last task looming over me. I still hadn't decided if reaching my Destination was a good thing or a bad thing and Hayden's insistence that it was important wasn't doing much to comfort me.

Then, of course, there was the matter of our kiss the night before. I wasn't quite sure how Hayden would handle the potentially awkward social situation today, but I knew that I was handling it exactly how I wanted to: curled up in bed, hiding from the world.

Hayden wasn't really the doting, romantic, boyfriend type. I wasn't under the impression that he'd suddenly be all cuddly and sweet. In fact, I would have worried about his sanity if he was. Of course that being said, I had absolutely no idea what to expect from a post-kiss Hayden. I wasn't even sure how *I* felt about everything that had happened last night. Yes, I had wanted to kiss Hayden, no matter how much I tried to deny it, but that didn't mean that I *should* have kissed him.

What could I possibly gain from doing that?

Today was my last task and I knew he couldn't come with me wherever I was going, so I had just unintentionally complicated my last cycle over one stupid kiss.

Well, one amazing kiss I guess. But still, that didn't make it okay.

The light had long-since faded from my window, replaced by fog, and yet I still made no move to get out of bed and Hayden hadn't come knocking yet. It looked like we were both avoiding the "morning after" scenario.

In a perfect world, Hayden would come storming into the room, sweep me off my feet into a kiss, and tell me how wonderful I was and how happy he was that we had finally wordlessly declared our feelings for each other.

But something told me that wasn't going to happen.

As if on cue, the front door swung open and Hayden swaggered in, looking like his normal smug self, and not giving any signs that last night had even happened.

"You're still in bed. Perfect," he said, and even without looking at him, I could hear the implied eye roll there.

I didn't want to deal with this. Instead of being an adult, I rolled over onto my side so that I faced the wall and all Hayden had, was a view of my back. Take that Mr. "I'm too dark and brooding to ever have feelings for anyone other than myself and my own twisty darkness."

"Are you giving up now that we're on the last task? Because so help me, I will march you through that maze at gunpoint if I have to," he threatened, taking a few steps closer to me and pulling the quilt off of the bed in one swift movement.

"While I have no doubt that you'll live up to your threat, I don't feel like getting up right now," I protested, still keeping my back to him. "I'm not sure I even want to reach my Destination yet."

"Fantastic," he deadpanned, before sliding his arms under me and lifting me off the bed.

He held me like a baby as he carried me from the cabin, bringing me across a brick floor.

"Let me go, Hayden! You can't force me to do the task!" I shouted, pounding his chest with my fists.

"On the contrary. You're kind of small and puny, while *I* am much bigger than you and completely capable of forcing you to do whatever I want," he said matter-of-factly, coming to a stop at the top of a large brick staircase that looked out over the biggest brick maze I had ever seen.

He dumped me unceremoniously onto the ground and I couldn't help but feel like not only were we ignoring the kiss last night, we had also regressed back to the way we treated each other the very first day we'd met. That wasn't exactly a good thing. It meant a lot more bruises for me and a lot more frustration for Hayden.

I rubbed my backside as I stood up and glared at my Guide angrily.

"I don't know how many times I can tell you this, but you're the worst human being I've ever met," I told him.

"That's great. Now get a good look at the maze, because this is the only time you'll get to see it," he said, completely unfazed by my statement. "Task six: Memory."

"Memory… as in how well I can use my memory while being chased by some terrible monster? Or just… memory?"

"No chasing. No potential dismemberment. Just try to

remember where that little marker in the middle of the maze is and how to get there or we're going to be stuck together for a long time today. And trust me love, I don't really fancy that at the moment."

Oh yeah, he was *definitely* not the cuddly boyfriend type.

Mustering the pieces of my completely shredded pride, I stuck my chin out and tried to look like I didn't care about how mean Hayden was being, all the while taking in the maze below me. If he wanted to get away from me that was just fine. I could complete the task quickly, finally reach my Destination, and be done with him. Talk about good motivation for going to the Other Side. Hayden's repellant personality was better than any zombie.

"Piece of cake," I said confidently. No way was I going to play the wounded cast-off girlfriend role.

"Glad you're so confident and everything, but do try to take this task seriously. It's not as easy as it looks."

I huffed at Hayden but took his advice, really trying to memorize the maze in front of me. The entire thing was made from bright red bricks that formed a giant circular maze with a brick marker in the middle. It was actually pretty intimidating from where I stood.

I tried to memorize directions in my mind but after a

while my "first right, second left, next left," directions became too complicated. It was just a maze, I was sure I could figure it out.

"Ready?" Hayden asked, looking over at me with absolutely no faith.

I narrowed my eyes at him then proceeded to walk down the stairs, leaving him in my wake.

A large wooden door marked the entrance to the labyrinth and I took a deep breath before opening it, hoping Hayden hadn't been lying about the "no monsters" clause of this task. I could easily see him getting great joy out of casting me as the unsuspecting prey of some mythological maze-guarding Minotaur.

The door closed behind Hayden and me once we entered the maze, casting us into relative silence. The brick walls and floors mixed with the foggy air made the entire place a bit cold and dreary but I resisted the urge to shiver, and simply turned right to begin my journey.

The soft skin of my fingers traced the rough brick wall as I walked, remembering at least the first few turns I was supposed to make before my memory completely failed me.

A memory test was probably the hardest task I could have encountered. I had an awful memory when I was alive, and something told me now that I was dead it was probably even worse.

Head trauma had a tendency to do that.

After about thirty minutes of walking blindly through the maze and backtracking a few times, Hayden looked over at me with a satisfied grin and said, "Lost?"

"I'm not lost," I protested, trying to think of a better way to say I had no idea where I was going. "I'm just…," I let my words trail off.

"Lost?" Hayden offered again, wrinkling his nose up in a move that would have been cute if it wasn't so frustrating.

"Ugh. I hate you so much," I said for the millionth time since I'd met him. "And I'm not lost."

"Right," he said, not buying it for a second. "I suppose you wanted to walk down this path that leads to a dead end."

I didn't want to believe that he was right, but glancing around the corner and coming into contact with yet another brick wall, I let out a frustrated sigh and turned on my heel to backtrack.

"After you," he said, placing his hand gently on my lower back as he ushered me away from the dead end.

I gave him an odd look, wondering why he was touching me at all but he didn't seem to notice.

We continued on like that for quite some time: exchanging snaky remarks, not really getting anywhere, and Hayden finding little reasons to put his hand on my arm or my back. It was completely confusing since he was blatantly refusing to talk about our kiss at all, yet here he was, sending me mixed signals.

I tried to ignore the knot in my stomach over my mysterious Destination, hoping the phrase "final destination" was a lot less sinister than it sounded. No matter how I justified it, however, I couldn't help but feel that it was unwise of me to so willingly go to this Destination on the word of a crazy man.

"Not quite," Hayden said as we rounded another corner and found yet another dead end.

I didn't say anything to his triumphant exclamation this time; instead I rolled my eyes silently and walked in the other direction with Hayden, yet again, placing his hand on my back.

"Why do you keep doing that?" I finally asked him, fed up with all of the mysteries in my life.

"It's fun to see that little vein stand out on your forehead when I make you mad," he replied with a sideways smile.

"Not *that*," I said, nodding over my shoulder to the

dead end where he'd made fun of me. "Why do you keep touching me?"

At my words his smile instantly vanished and he quickly dropped his hand from my back. It was almost as if he hadn't realized he was touching me and bringing it to his attention had embarrassed him.

"I'm not touching you," he said, even though it was incredibly obvious that he'd dropped his hand away from me.

"Okay," I said mockingly.

I shook my head as I walked through the brick maze, unable to remember if I'd already gone this way or not. Hayden had hung back for a moment and now jogged to catch up to me.

"Why do you think I've been touching you?" he asked, and for a moment it sounded like he was asking what I thought his intention was.

It didn't take long for me to realize he was asking why I was imagining that he had been touching me. Like I was making the whole thing up.

Frustrated, I stopped in my tracks and turned to face him.

"All day you've been touching my elbow," I said, grabbing his elbow in demonstration. "Or putting your hand on my back." Again I demonstrated this by placing my other hand on his lower back, trying to make a point by making him as uncomfortable as his weird physical contact had made me. "Why do you keep doing that?" I practically shouted.

"You're nuts," he said, pulling away from me and looking like he pitied me. "Maybe I've been trying to help you today. Why is that such a big deal?"

I knew I wasn't the one who was crazy. Hayden hadn't ever touched me before, and now that we'd kissed he suddenly found any excuse to be close. This wouldn't have been weird if he would have just acknowledged our kiss from the night before. The fact that he was completely against bringing it up at all just made this entire exchange uncomfortable.

"Just forget it," I said, making my way through the maze once more, completely lost and now just hoping I'd accidentally find the marker in the middle. "I wish I had some lipstick."

"Lipstick?" Hayden asked warily.

"So I could mark which way I've already gone," I explained. "I saw it in a movie once."

"And it's always a safe bet to get your strategies from movies," he said sarcastically.

"You know what? I wasn't asking you for your permission or advice, I was just mentioning something. You don't have to weigh in on every little thing I say because honestly, I don't really care what you think," I snapped.

The silence that followed my little outburst seemed to last forever and all I could hear was my own ragged breathing. How did this man make me so mad all the time?

"Are you finished now?" he asked in a bored tone. "Because we really should be getting on with things."

I widened my eyes at his lack of tact and went on with the task, trying to ignore my Guide all together.

When I'd been standing over the maze, scoping the whole thing out, it hadn't looked quite as big as it did now, and the longer we walked, the more tired I became. I remembered being amazed during the first task that I didn't get fatigued as the zombie chased me through the woods. Now, I was simply walking through a brick maze and it seemed to be too much for me.

I wanted to ask Hayden what the explanation for this little anomaly was, but didn't want to break my vow of silence towards him. He needed to know that he couldn't be terrible and rude all the time without consequences.

"Are you being so weird today because of what

happened last night?" Hayden asked, completely surprising me.

I hadn't expected him to be the one to breach the subject. Not in a million years.

"No," I lied, still walking and trying to ignore how tired I was.

"Because that was just… a moment of poor judgment," he said, showing an even more stunning lack of tact than I thought possible from him.

And that was saying something.

"Agreed," I said shortly, refusing to look at him.

"So we should probably just forget about the whole thing," he went on, quite unnecessarily.

"I said 'agreed'. Would you just stop talking?"

It was incredible that he could make an already bad and awkward situation so much worse in just a few seconds. Now, not only was I mad at him for ignoring the kiss, I was furious that when he did acknowledge it, he made it sound like a mistake he regretted.

Wonderful. Some "special moment" we had shared.

"I'm just saying, I'm your Guide and it doesn't look great if there appears to be something going on between us," he went on, not listening to my request to be quiet.

"Good thing there's absolutely nothing going on,

huh?" I asked, unable to hide the irritation in my voice.

"Exactly," he said, though his heart wasn't in it.

He was all about giving me mixed signals.

"Actually… Isla," Hayden began, though I quickly cut him off.

"There it is!" I exclaimed, running over to the tall brick pillar at the center of the maze.

My feet splashed through a small puddle of water right in front of the pillar and Hayden's strong grip wrapped around my upper arm as he pulled me backwards; a habit he couldn't seem to break.

"Ouch!" I yelled, yanking my arm out of his iron grip.

"Stop whining, I just saved you," he said in annoyance, pointing to the puddle I had been running through.

At the center of the water was a dark, square hole, as if a chimney had been submerged under a pond.

"What is that thing?" I asked, suddenly glad that Hayden had so forcefully pulled me away.

"That's for you," he said, actually sounding very worried and not at all like he was happy I had another impossible task in front of me. "How long can you hold your breath?"

CHAPTER 20

"What?" I asked.

This seemed to be how a lot of our conversations went. Hayden would tell me something I didn't want to hear, I would question him, then I'd end up doing whatever it was anyway because I either wanted to get *away* from Hayden or get *to* him. Today I still hadn't quite made up my mind on which motivation I was utilizing.

"This is the last part of the task before you reach your Destination," he explained, looking like he didn't even want to tell me what I had to do.

He had gone from saying he didn't want anything to do with me, to worrying about me in about five seconds. I was starting to worry he might have multiple personalities.

"And what exactly is that?" I asked.

"Underwater here, there's a tunnel that leads to a grate. On the other side of the grate is your Destination."

"And I have to swim there?" I guessed, looking at the chimney-like structure underwater and thinking there was no way I could swim through that space.

Really, there wouldn't even be enough room for me to paddle underwater, I'd just have to propel myself down the tunnel using my hands on the walls. The idea gave me goose bumps… and not the good kind.

"You'll probably want to get into the water head first, that way you can see where you're going since the space is too small to turn your body around once inside," he said mechanically.

"I can't go in there," I said, suddenly feeling claustrophobic at the thought of the dark tunnel filled with water.

Not only would I have to go in head first, I'd have to swim straight down, away from the air at the surface of the tunnel. That didn't bode well when you were swimming away from the air.

"What if I run out of oxygen?" I asked, feeling utterly panicked at the idea of completing this task.

I wished Hayden would have told me about this task before I'd completed the other ones. I would have just stayed back on the floating islands forever, happy as could be.

"I suggest you move quickly," he said. "Once you're completely submerged, a grate will close off the entrance of the tunnel so you can't backtrack even if you want to."

"Wait. So not only will I be moving through a small water-filled tunnel with no air, but I can't come back to get air if I run out? I only have one shot to do this?"

My knees began to shake and suddenly I needed to sit down. I let myself fall onto the hard brick floor, my boots beginning to soak through where my feet touched the dark water.

"Once you get to the end of the tunnel, you just have to open the grate and swim through, then you'll reach your Destination," he went on, acting like he was unfazed by this task though I could see that he didn't want me to do it.

"How far away from the entrance is the grate?" I asked, looking up at Hayden and feeling a few involuntary tears streak my cheeks.

I could deal with monsters, and cliffs, and rogue arrows, but I wasn't sure I could deal with a cold, dark, space where I was likely to drown with no hope for escape.

"I don't know," he said. "I'm sorry."

And in his defense, he actually sounded like he was.

"Hayden, please don't make me do this," I pleaded, not caring that I looked weak and he'd probably make fun of me. “Please. I’ll do something else. Some other task.”

He shook his head, but didn’t look at me. Instead he stared at a spot on the floor, clenching his jaw and shifting his weight. Something was making him uncomfortable. Maybe having actual human feelings when faced with a weeping girl?

“I’ll fight some kind of monster or complete another puzzle. Just please don’t make me go in there. I can’t do the small-spaces-and-no-air thing.”

“It’s not up to me,” he said, now looking down at me apologetically.

At least in my last moments, I got to be with “sort of nice Hayden”, rather than the normal grouchy version of himself he portrayed so flawlessly.

“Hayden, I’m scared. I can’t do this.”

It sounded like I was begging him to fix it for me, and really, I kind of was. At this point I wasn’t too proud to beg.

Tapping his thumb against his leg he came to some sort of decision, extending his hand and pulling me back onto my feet. He grabbed me by both arms, holding me at a distance and looking at me intently as if trying to get his message across.

“Isla, I’m going to be straight with you,” he began.

“When I first met you, I was really mad that we’d been paired up because I really didn’t want another failure on my hands.”

I wasn’t sure what part of this speech was supposed to make me feel better, but I let him continue, not wanting to cut him off.

“I was convinced that you were weak, spoiled, and completely unmotivated. I was positive you wouldn’t make it past the first task, so I didn’t let myself get too invested in you.” His words were hard to hear, no matter how true they were. “But then you made it past the first task. And then the second. And then the third, until finally, you had gotten through all of them and you were at the last task.

“You’ll have to forgive me for having absolutely no faith in you until it was so obvious that I should have. I can be a bit dense sometimes,” he said, giving me the sideways smirk he had worn the night before, when all of the confused feelings had started.

“I wouldn’t jump the gun,” I told him, wiping the tears from my cheeks and trying to buck up a little. “You probably shouldn’t have too much faith in me right now. I don’t think I’ll be completing this task.”

“You don’t give yourself enough credit. I know I’m your harshest critic and I haven’t done anything to make this whole experience easier on you. But despite my best efforts to keep you from your goal, you've reached it anyway. You're a lot stronger than you think, and this last task isn't anything you can't handle."

I wasn't sure where the motivational speech had come from, but I would be lying if I said it didn't make me feel at least slightly more hopeful about reaching my Destination safely.

You know, without drowning first.

With Hayden's track record, however, I did have to wonder if the sudden burst of motivation was spurred on by his own desire to succeed. Just as he'd buttered me up during the second task just to force me to jump off of the island, he could very easily be playing the part of "supportive Guide" just to make me complete this task.

"As touching as it is that you have faith in me, I still can't do this Hayden. I'd rather just sit here until I fail rather than dying in a watery death chamber," I admitted, not sure how I felt about Hayden being here to see the moment I completely lost my pride and gave up all together.

"Isla, you're so close. You just have to take a leap of faith and do it."

"A leap of faith I'd be fine with. Give me any sort of

ledge and I'll jump… as long as I'm not jumping into water. Besides, I still don't know that I want to reach my Destination. We don't know what's waiting on the other side for me. All we know is you won't be going with me."

"I'd think that would be a perk. Sort of a reward for passing all of the tasks," he said with a grin that made my legs feel all wobbly.

"Sometimes I feel like it would be a reward," I began. "And then you'll show me a little sympathy, and suddenly I remember why I ever thought of you as a friend in the first place. I just wish you'd be a little more consistent."

"Where's the fun in that?" he asked with a raise of his thick eyebrow.

I laughed at his statement and nodded. At some point in time I'd have to stop talking to Hayden and actually force myself to get inside of the small, water-filled chamber at my feet. I just wanted to put it off as long as I could.

"Since I'm probably about to die again anyway, and I'm sure I'll never see you after this, can you answer me one question?" I asked. "Without any sarcasm or joking or hidden agenda."

"Doesn't really sound like something I would agree to, but I guess if this is your dying wish I can grant it," he said, garnering a dirty look from me. "Just kidding. You aren't going to die in there… now what's your question?"

"Why did you kiss me?" I asked.

Hayden looked taken aback by the query, though I couldn't believe he hadn't seen it coming. I wanted the honest answer from him, though I still wasn't sure if I was hoping he'd tell me he hated me so I wouldn't have anything to lose in that tunnel, or if he'd tell me he liked me so that I had a reason to be brave.

"I kissed you because, for one moment, I let myself be unprofessional and unbridled, no matter what the consequences were and no matter what the outcome of that kiss was," he said honestly, his hands still grasping my arms.

"And?"

"And it was the most terrifying thing I've ever done. It was awful and wonderful all at the same time," he explained with a laugh. "I'm not really the type of person to be ruled by my emotions."

"Except your anger," I pointed out.

"Except for that," he agreed.

"So why did you say it was a moment of poor judgment earlier?" I asked, needing to know before I took the plunge into my watery grave. Somehow it made a difference to me, despite the fact that, in the scheme of things, it didn't matter to my overall success in this task.

"Oh, I don't know," he said, rubbing the back of his neck after dropping my arms. "Because you hadn't said anything about it and it looked like you were avoiding me that morning, so I didn't want to be the creepy guy who'd taken advantage of your exhausted state last night, then kept pushing the matter the next morning. And I suppose my ego was a bit hurt that you'd avoided me."

I hadn't thought for one moment that I'd avoided Hayden that morning, but looking back on the day, my refusal to get out of bed or talk to him was a bit avoidant. Maybe he wasn't the only one with a stunning lack of tact.

"I did kind of do that, didn't I?" I asked guiltily.

"Just a bit," he agreed. "Listen, I'm sorry I've been so hard on you, but you really have done beautifully here. I don't have a doubt in my mind that you'll make it through that tunnel just fine."

I didn't share his confidence but I couldn't tell him that when he was actually being nice to me. And apparently he hadn't regretted our kiss as much as I'd thought.

Now I stood there, looking back and forth between Hayden and the tunnel, not quite sure what to do. It felt like I should say goodbye to him. Like maybe I should thank him for the help he did offer when he wasn't being awful, or give him a hug or a pat on the shoulder.

Something.

It didn't seem right to just turn away from this person who'd gone through so many experiences with me in such a short time.

Not knowing what I should do, I gave Hayden one last smile, lost for words, and walked towards the puddle. I removed my boots one final time, not wanting them to weigh me down, and tried not to shiver at the temperature of the chilly water.

"Isla, wait," Hayden called, splashing up beside me.

I turned to him expectantly. I knew he wasn't the romantic type but that didn't stop me from hoping he would make some sort of movie-worthy declaration of love… or at least, like.

Instead he pulled a small metal flashlight from his pocket and handed it over.

"It's not very bright, but it's better than a pitch black hole," he said, not sounding very enthusiastic.

"Thanks," I responded, taking the flashlight from him and giving him a little halfhearted smile. "And thanks for your help with everything."

"You have an odd idea of what the word 'help' means, but I'll take it," he joked, using my own earlier accusation against me.

"Goodbye, Hayden," I said. "I'll miss the English accent."

He laughed at my statement, nodding fondly over the memory.

"I may not miss your Southern accent but I'll miss you… just a little," he admitted, bringing his finger and thumb together to show just how little he'd miss me.

I wrapped my arms around his neck and pulled him in for a hug, not wanting to say goodbye to him forever without at least some sort of affection shown. It wasn't easy being stuck with him for so long, but I'd learned a lot about my own strength and I had to give him credit for that.

"You'll be great," he said in my ear, hugging me back tightly.

"That was actually a nice thing to say," I accused, pulling away but still holding his arms.

"Try not to screw it up like you've screwed everything else up," he quickly amended.

"That's more like it," I said, leaning over in a moment of extremely uncharacteristic bravery and planting a small kiss on his lips.

It lasted only a second and neither one of us said anything when I pulled away. Hayden smiled fondly at me, looking like he'd set aside all of the things he didn't like about me for one minute so we could enjoy this nice moment. I didn't want to drag things on any longer, already losing what little nerve I had, so instead of saying goodbye again I turned away from him, flashlight clutched tightly in my hand and looked down at the dark water beneath me.

"Courage, Isla," Hayden whispered in my ear, his lips brushing against my temple as he spoke.

I turned around quickly, suddenly wondering if we could just stay in the final task together without ever having to worry about possible suffocation, but he was gone.

There was no trace that he'd ever even been there.

The immediate feeling of emptiness was overwhelming, but it did help me get on with the task. If Hayden had stuck around it was possible I would have made excuses to sit and talk with him forever.

"Right," I said, giving myself a mental shake and facing the tunnel once more. "You just have to do it."

And with that, I got on my knees, took a deep breath, and fell head first into the small, water-filled passageway.

CHAPTER 21

What little light the small opening to the passageway produced was instantly extinguished as the grate slid closed over my only source of oxygen. My slippery hand held the flashlight in front of me while the other hand pressed against the brick walls that surrounded me on all sides, propelling me downward through the darkness.

It wasn't a good sign that the only thing I saw ahead of me was a brick wall dead end quite a ways away. That, combined with the fact that I'd never been able to hold my breath for very long, were quickly making the panic set in. I could feel my heart racing, and suddenly I had to wonder if this whole thing had been a terrible idea.

Maybe I'd been right to question the appeal of reaching my Destination. Maybe all it really meant was I was dying again. It didn't make much sense for that to be the case; even in my panicked, air-deprived state I could see that. Still, I felt an ominous sense of foreboding as I floated down the tunnel, going ever deeper underground.

By the time I reached the other side of the tunnel, my body was involuntarily gulping, trying to get the nonexistent air into my lungs. All of my muscles seemed to be tensing at once and I desperately looked around for the grate Hayden had told me about. Instead, all I found was another long, watery hallway with no end in sight.

My eyes widened at the implications of this new hallway and had I been in the open air rather than trapped underwater, I probably would have cried. Instead I pushed my feet desperately off of the brick wall, hoping that the fact that this new hallway was going to the side and not downward anymore was a good sign.

I was in full meltdown mode in a matter of seconds. I could see another brick wall looming ever closer ahead of me, which meant another endless passageway to swim through with no air, but it was likely I didn't even have enough air left in my lungs to reach the next brick wall at all. I was growing weaker by the second from the emotional day I'd had, and the sheer fact that I hadn't taken a breath in an unhealthy amount of time.

Desperate, I shone the flashlight all over the passageway, hoping there would be some sort of hidden compartment in the wall or a reset button I could push. The beam of my light pierced the murky water dully and though the reset button was nowhere to be found, I saw a small indent in the ceiling, where a tiny pocket of air had been trapped. Even though it seemed far-fetched, I hoped I'd be able to breathe it in. At this point I was open to any and all possibilities.

I plugged my nose with my free hand to avoid drowning myself, rolled over onto my back in the passageway, and pressed my lips to the small air pocket. The dry brick, though rough against my skin, was a welcome sensation and I tried to maintain my cool as I slowly sucked the air into my mouth. I didn't want to gasp suddenly and end up filling my lungs with water by accident.

The air was stale but it stopped my body's trembling momentarily and it gave me the boost I needed to get to the other side of the tunnel. With the newfound motivation of fresh air in my lungs I continued my sideways journey to the next seemingly dead end.

This time, instead of a tunnel leading even further away from hope, the next open passageway was above me, leading up towards a light far away. If my air-deprived brain was working correctly, it seemed like I had swam in a giant "U" shape and would open the grate to find myself somewhere inside of the maze still. It didn't seem like I'd swam far enough to get me completely out of the endless sprawling brick structure.

Ignoring this fact and focusing on getting to the air above me, I pushed off of the bricks, hopefully for the last time, with my hand stretched out in front of me, grasping for the distant grate.

I scrambled frantically through the passageway that seemed to get narrower and narrower the closer I got to the grate. The little flashlight slipped out of my hand in the struggle and I was instantly engulfed in a partial darkness. Luckily, the grate above me gave off enough light to lead me in the right direction, no matter how eerie the sudden darkness was.

My palms scraped against the rough bricks as I tried to fight my desire to take a breath, just like I had the time I'd sat beside my own body, watching my brother Tuck trying to revive me. As I neared the grate up ahead, I had to readjust my hands. The passageway had become too narrow to keep my arms at my sides and from that point on, I'd need to raise my arms above my head in order to fit through the small space.

To say that I felt claustrophobic with the walls literally

closing in on me would be an understatement.

I could feel the skin on my shoulders getting scratched up as I wiggled my body through the space, hoping it wouldn't get any narrower before I reached the grate. My upward progression was already slow and soon enough, I'd have to come to a complete stop. That wasn't an option I wanted to explore any time soon.

I used my fingertips to inch myself forward until my body stopped all together, just out of reach of the grate. I was completely wedged between the four brick walls with my arms pinned over my head, waving around helplessly right beneath the grate.

My heartbeat quickened, and my eyes began rolling back into my head as my lungs screamed for air. I could feel myself losing control over my body and I knew that I'd slip into unconsciousness any moment and drown in this terrifying space.

I tried to push myself just a few more inches with my feet. With my bare toes dragging across the bricks, I was able to move my body a good two inches closer to the grate above me, still only one inch out of reach. The water in front of me was tinted a faint shade of pink, and I could only imagine the damage I'd done to my shoulders when I'd pushed myself further up the tunnel. I could feel the brick tearing into my skin with every attempt to push myself closer to the grate, but a few scratches were the least of my worries with my world quickly darkening around me.

Utilizing my last bit of strength, I pushed off the brick wall one last time with my toes, hoping it would get me to my Destination.

My cold fingers made contact with the grate in front of me and as I wrapped them around the metal, I could feel the open air just above me. Sadly, I was still stuck.

The irony of drowning only inches away from the surface of the water was not lost on me, though I wished I could have been enjoying it from the topside of this disaster.

Holding on to the grate as tightly as I could, I tried to push it to the side.

Unfortunately, that happened to be the exact same moment my body gave up on me and as the grate began to slide, my world went black.

CHAPTER 22

"I swear I saw it," I heard Tuck say somewhere far away.

His voice was muffled and distant but it was distinctly his and I had to wonder if I was making things up again, or if I was allowed to hear their voices one last time before passing over for good.

I was acutely aware of the fact that my entire body throbbed and my head ached, but I could care less about the pain in my body right at that particular moment, because I could actually breathe. Somehow I'd managed to get through the grate, even though I didn't remember doing it.

Really, based on the last thing I remembered, I probably shouldn't have completed the task. I was wedged between the brick walls and completely out of air. That entire scenario just reeked of a bad ending.

Yet here I was, in some fuzzy dark place hearing the voice of my brother. No matter how much my body ached, hearing his voice made going through all of the impossible tasks worth it.

"Son, I didn't see anything," my dad replied, sounding a bit closer than Tuck.

"I saw her eyelids move, Dad," Tuck insisted.

His voice was losing the fuzzy quality and had become sharp and clear.

"Go get your mother," Daddy instructed, and a second later I heard his retreating footsteps.

So this was it? I got to see my entire family before I left? Maybe passing on wouldn't be nearly as traumatizing as I'd thought. Somewhere deep inside of me I wished Hayden would be part of my welcoming committee (or was it more like a farewell committee?) but I'd gotten to spend a lot of time with him those past few days. I could understand if he didn't want to see me again already.

"Isla?" my mom called, and suddenly I felt her hand brushing against my arm.

The gesture actually hurt quite a bit, which I hadn't expected, and it made me flinch.

"Did you see that?" Tuck asked incredulously.

I lifted the corner of my mouth in the smallest hint of a smile at my brother's antics. It was amazing that the smallest gesture on my part seemed so interesting to him.

"She's smiling!" my mom practically shouted.

The apparently monumental task of smiling quickly wore me out and I let the expression fade from my face. If I couldn't even smile for more than a few seconds, how was I supposed to open my eyes? I'd managed to make it through six impossible tasks with an impossible man, hardly ever breaking a sweat, and now I couldn't even smile?

"Baby, can you hear me?" she asked.

Despite the exhaustion I felt, I slowly opened my eyes, wondering what my heavenly surroundings would look like and excited to see my family one last time.

Blinding white lights directly above me made me flinch the second I opened my eyes, which in turn hurt my head, so I quickly closed them again.

"She's awake. She's really awake," Daddy said, sounding choked up over this revelation.

The emotion in his voice made me wish I could do something more impressive than just opening my eyes for two seconds. I wanted to sit up and give him a hug, or tell him to stop worrying because I was fine now and I'd watch over him from heaven. Instead, I settled for opening my eyes once more, determined not to close them again.

The world went in and out of focus, the lights were too

bright, and the faces of my family seemed entirely too tired and worried. Each one of them looked like they hadn't slept in years, but they were happy anyway. That was a sentiment I could relate to. Despite my exhaustion it felt amazing to finally see them again.

"Isla, can you hear me?" my mom asked slowly, her voice much too loud for my headache.

I tried to tell her I was fine. I opened my mouth to form the words but no sound came out. It was just too tiring.

"Don't tire her out, Molly," my dad said, never taking his eyes off of me. "They said she'd tire easily when she woke up."

I blinked my eyes a few times, trying to get rid of the blurriness. It was odd seeing my parents again when I'd thought they were gone forever, but it was even odder to have them talking about me when I was laying right there.

Since it seemed like the only thing I could do without wanting to collapse into a heap was move my eyes, I let them wander around the room that was anything but heavenly. I tried to make sense of what I was seeing and suddenly, I wasn't so positive that I had died.

I was lying in a hospital room with machines whirring and beeping all around me. The smell was sterile, the lights were far too bright, but it definitely wasn't heaven.

But nothing about this situation made any sense. If I hadn't died, where had I been before this? Had I been stuck in some sort of limbo while my body decided if it was going to die or not? And what did that make Hayden? The angel of death?

My mind was completely overloaded with questions and nothing seemed to make sense. All I wanted to do was ask my parents what was going on, yet I couldn't even form a sentence. Maybe I had died and this was what hell was like; all sorts of questions with no way to answer them.

Trying to set aside my frustration at the lack of control I had over my voice, I tested out the rest of my body. It took some effort, and my bones felt stiff, but I was able to wiggle my fingers and toes a bit. In fact, it seemed like I would have been able to move all of my muscles if only I wasn't so tired.

"Tuck, go wake up the doctor," my dad instructed.

Wake them up? I guessed if it was late at night that would explain the tired looks on my family's faces. How long had I been unconscious? I'd crashed my truck pretty late, so really it could have been any span of time. Two hours, maybe four or five before the sun came up?

As Tuck disappeared, I attempted to lift my arm up,

remembering the horrific scene in the cab of my truck after it had crashed. There'd been so much blood. How had I survived that and what on earth did I look like now?

"Honey, just try to rest," my mom said, glancing down at my hand that I was desperately trying to lift.

I knew she was right. I knew I needed to take it easy, but I had to see if my face was completely gone or something else equally as awful.

It took all of my strength, but I managed to bring my hand up to my face, feeling the sore skin there. I gingerly ran my fingers over the place that gave me the most pain: the left side of my forehead, right at my hairline. My eyes widened as I felt the bristly stitches poking through my skin and my mom instantly grabbed my hand and pulled it away.

What did I look like and why couldn't I talk? Was I forever damaged because of that stupid dog in the road? I should have just waited until I got home to listen to my new CD. My mind instantly filled with even more questions and I suddenly felt dizzy, like my entire hospital bed had suddenly turned to one side and was about to dump me onto the floor.

"Just relax," my mom soothed, looking over at my dad who, in turn, looked behind the curtain at the bed next to mine.

Why was he looking at the patient next to me?

"Is he awake?" Daddy asked Tuck, who suddenly reappeared.

Even my doctor was sleeping in the room with me? I must have been in pretty bad shape to warrant around-the-clock surveillance.

"Yeah," he answered simply, nodding at the doctor as he approached.

"Dr. Temple, she's moving around but she still hasn't said anything," my dad informed the man on the other side of the curtain.

It didn't escape my notice that he'd called him Dr. Temple and I involuntarily held my breath, waiting to see if he was who I thought he'd be, or if my imagination had made him up all together.

"That's to be expected at first Mr. Edison," the doctor told him with a thick English accent, bringing my heart rate up a few more notches, which normally wouldn't have been embarrassing, but the beeping machine next to me sped up as well. Talk about humiliating. "It'll take her a bit to get acclimated and we won't know just how difficult it will be for her to recover until we test things out."

A second later he was by my bed side, sporting blue

scrubs and a white lab coat rather than the all-black ensemble he'd worn during the tasks. He looked exactly the same as he had when I'd kissed him only moments before that, though his eyes seemed more tired and his face was a little scruffier.

"Miss Edison? Can you blink twice if you can hear me?" he asked, looking down at me with a look of concern, his thick eyebrows knitted together.

It was Hayden. My Hayden.

I blinked twice and attempted a smile at him, though I wasn't sure what it actually ended up looking like.

Did he remember me? Or had I completely made up a relationship with him through pieces of conversation I'd heard in my unconscious state?

"Why does she look like that?" Tuck suddenly asked.

"Tucker!" my mom reprimanded.

"What, Momma? She's got a weird look on her face."

"Ah, yes well...," Hayden began, looking a bit flustered. Maybe he did remember me and was now embarrassed that he'd have to tell my family how terrible he always was to me. "She might be experiencing some confusion as she tries to cope with what she experienced while in the coma and what she's seeing now."

Coma?

"Miss Edison," Hayden said slowly. "You were in a car accident three weeks ago."

My brain went fuzzy again as the room tilted to one side. Three weeks? I'd been in a coma for three weeks?

"You've got a broken arm that's still healing and you had a pretty nasty head wound but you've been healing up beautifully. You were in a coma for that period of time but we have high hopes for your recovery."

Oh yeah, there was no way this was my Hayden. He was being way too gentle. If it was *my* Hayden he'd say, "You got hurt. It's no big deal. Why don't you just suck it up and stop whining?" But did that mean I had completely made him up and now I was stuck with feelings for someone who I hadn't actually spent any time with?

"I," I said, trying desperately to form a sentence. My brain was just so fuzzy.

My mom's eyes widened at this attempt. Apparently they hadn't expected me to be able to speak. I'm sure Hayden would have been fine if I never spoke again since I bothered him so much with my incessant whining, but that would only be true if this guy really was who I remembered.

"That's great, Miss Edison," Hayden said encouragingly, freaking me out to no end with the "nice guy" act.

Even if this wasn't really my Hayden, it was odd to see someone who looked exactly like him acting so nice and responsible.

"Stitches?" I asked, and instantly my brother burst out in laughter, causing my mom to hit him on the arm for his outburst.

"Leave it to my sister to ask about her looks first thing," Tuck said, still laughing and smiling at me fondly.

I'd missed him, and it felt amazing to actually see his face again. Tuck just *got* me.

"I won't bother you with the details of your injuries since they're healing quite well," Hayden began, still sounding much too professional.

"Your scalp was kind of pulled away from your head," my brother elaborated, and while normally I'd be grateful for his honestly, at that moment it just made my stomach turn.

"Son," my dad said warningly.

Even Hayden gave him a disapproving look.

There it was. Seeing him look like he disapproved of something was much more familiar.

"That's not important right now. What *is* important is that by the time you're healed, you'll just have a small scar along your hairline. Not much bigger than the one on the nape of your neck."

For a moment I was convinced that this one statement proved that Hayden had been real the whole time. I'd told him the story of when I'd hit my head on the rock in the river and had gotten a scar on the nape of my neck. How else would he know about that?

Unless of course he was my doctor and had examined me and seen the scar… which was the more likely explanation.

"The best thing for Miss Edison right now is rest. It's a good sign that she's speaking a bit, but we don't want to overwhelm her."

My mom looked like she wasn't about to get kicked out of the room by a doctor, but Hayden gave her a meaningful look that, apparently, overruled her desire to be with me.

"You guys will want to be well rested when you see her tomorrow. I think a good night's rest in your own beds will do you a world of good."

"But," Momma began.

"I'm here all night and I promise I'll check in on her so excessively that the nurses will worry about my sanity," he assured her with a smile.

I didn't want my family to leave already. My heart ached at the thought of being away from them again.

"Thank you, Dr. Temple," my mom said gratefully, looking over at me with a warm smile.

They continued to talk about me while I laid there motionless, and I tried desperately to tell them that I wasn't tired and didn't want to go to sleep, but my eyelids involuntarily closed and no matter what I tried to tell myself about how awake I was, I let sleep take me.

CHAPTER 23

Despite how tired I was, my sleep was restless and sporadic. I kept waking with a start and had to make sense of my surroundings when I found myself in a hospital room instead of a safe house.

It felt like I'd been alone in my hospital room for days, though the little digital clock on the wall informed me that my family had only been gone for a few hours. I couldn't seem to understand how I'd woken up seven or eight times in such a short time span, but eventually, I got bored with being alone and tried to make myself speak.

There was no way I was going to face Hayden again without being able to ask him some serious questions. Plus it would be nice to actually tell my family I was okay so they'd stop worrying so much about me.

I took a deep breath, gathering my thoughts and thinking my sentence through over and over again. It shouldn't have been so hard to utter one simple sentence, but suddenly it seemed like a monumental task.

"My name," I began, trying to form each word perfectly. "Is Isla Edison."

There.

That wasn't so hard.

Granted it had taken all of my brain power to say one sentence, not to mention how long the build-up to that one sentence had been. Still, it was much better than not being able to talk at all, and with a broken arm and stitches in my forehead, I'd cut my losses and take what I could get.

"My name is Isla Edison," I said again, this time with no pause in the middle.

That was definitely an improvement. It still didn't quite flow, but it was a complete sentence with no odd pauses. I was sure that with one more try I'd be able to master it.

"My name is--."

"Isla Edison," Hayden finished, coming in to the room with a clip board in his hand. "Yes. I heard you the first two times," he joked.

At the sight of my Guide who wasn't really my Guide I clammed up, suddenly unable to speak again.

"Sorry," he said quickly. "I didn't mean to startle you.

I just need to check a few things then I'll be out of your hair."

I nodded my head slowly (which I instantly regretted when I felt the shooting pains there) and followed his movements with my eyes.

He studied the various machines I was hooked up to, checked my IV bag, then placed his fingers over my wrist and looked down at his watch to check my pulse, even though I was hooked up to a machine that would tell him that exact thing. He was finding reasons to be close again. If this was really my Hayden. The feeling of his warm fingers on my cold skin sent little shivers through my body, and I suddenly felt a significant sense of loss over our relationship.

Even if the tasks were something I'd made up in my mind, I still felt like I knew him. It was a terrible feeling to look at someone so familiar, yet feel so distant from them. At that moment I would have given anything for him to say some rude or snarky comment to me, just so that I knew it was really my Hayden.

Instead he continued to scribble down notes on his clip board.

I gathered my thoughts together, trying to ask him a question. I wanted to be witty and funny. Maybe dry and sarcastic like he had always been, but all I managed was a pathetic, “Will I live, Dr. Temple.”

My question came out much too serious. I was trying to be lighthearted, but my broken speech just made it sound like I really thought I might die at any second. Not to mention the fact that the words “Dr. Temple” should never have escaped my lips. All the times I’d joked with Hayden about being a doctor, I’d never actually thought he was one.

Hayden couldn’t be something as serious as a doctor. He was just Hayden.

Still, I melted a little when he looked down at me with his blue eyes crinkling in the corners as he smiled.

“Yes, Miss Edison. You’ll live,” he assured me.

Miss Edison.

I hated the way he talked to me. So formal. It was just one more confirmation that whatever had happened to me for those three weeks in the coma were completely in my mind.

“We did an MRI when we first brought you in to rule out a subdural hematoma but it looks like you just had a concussion… though I’m still not sure why you slipped into a coma for so long, but the mind is a curious thing,” he said quickly, sounding so smart and important.

“English?” I asked with a small smile, which Hayden

returned.

"Right. We wanted to make sure you didn't have any bleeding in your brain or swelling that needed to be monitored, but you were fine," he began. "Although once I had a patient with some swelling and we had to take a piece of his skull off while we waited for the swelling to go down. To keep it viable we placed it in his abdomen," he finished, looking amused at the idea.

I crinkled my nose in disgust at his story.

"Sorry. Probably not very interesting if you aren't a doctor. I should have realized how gross that story is," he quickly said, backtracking and sounding a bit nervous.

He definitely wasn't talking to me with any familiarity. It almost seemed like he wasn't sure how he should act around me. It would have been cute if it wasn't so sad.

"I'll just…," he said, turning to leave and not finishing his sentence.

I watched Hayden walk to the door, but he stopped once he reached the doorway. His head turned from side to side as if examining the hallways before he slowly closed the bedroom door and came back to my bedside, taking a seat beside me.

He looked at me with a completely different expression than the ones I'd seen him wear since waking up. His brow was furrowed, his lips pursed, and he seemed troubled. He opened his mouth to speak but quickly shut it again, as if trying to think of how he should phrase whatever he had to say, and suddenly, I worried that I might actually be dying. Maybe he didn't want to say it in front of my family but I really only had a few more days to live.

Great.

I'd finally come to terms with the fact that I was alive after thinking I was dead all this time, and now I was just about to find out I really was about to die and I'd have to reassess everything *again*.

"Isla, do you remember me?" Hayden finally asked, still looking conflicted.

I looked over at him with wide eyes. What was he really asking me? My immediate thought was that everything was real and I really had experienced all of those terrifying and wonderful things with Hayden. But then I wondered if he was simply asking to make sure my short term memory was intact.

Unsure of how to answer, and hoping I could effectively convey my message when my speech was still so shaky, I kept my answer short and sweet. Thinking about what phrase would be vague enough that I wouldn't sound crazy if I had made everything up, yet still be specific enough that Hayden would know about everything if he really was who I thought he was, wasn't easy.

It was a monumental task to say the least.

"My Guide?" I asked, knitting my eyebrows together despite the fact that the skin on my forehead felt too tight.

Hayden's face instantly melted into a look of relief as he let out a breath I hadn't even realized he was holding. He nodded his head, a smile forming on his lips.

"What do you remember?" he asked.

That was a bit of a loaded question with only one easy answer.

"Everything," I said simply, hoping I didn't look too crazy at that moment.

I was completely over the moon with the thought that this was *my* Hayden. He remembered me. I didn't have to feel such a loss over our relationship.

"Why didn't you… say something before?" I asked, my speech much smoother, though I still had a few pauses I couldn't seem to control.

"I didn't think it would look very professional to hit on my patient in front of her family," he joked.

"If this is you… hitting on me I can… see why you're still single," I replied, feeling my lips curl up into a smile despite how sore my cheeks felt. "Skull in the abdomen?"

"Glad to see you haven't lost that classic Isla wit," he answered, sounding just like the Hayden I remembered, if not slightly nicer.

"You're certainly chipper," I accused, wondering why he wasn't being awful to me.

"About that," he began, looking guilty. "The whole procedure to bring you back apparently chose one aspect of my personality to cling to and that trait got exacerbated… a lot."

"You're really… a nice person?" I asked, hoping I could properly convey my skepticism through my broken speech.

"I'm a naturally dry and sarcastic person," he admitted. "And apparently when I transferred over, that turned into me being a sadistic jerk who tried to throw you off a cliff."

I giggled at the memory, though my ribs weren't too happy about the action.

"Thanks for that," I told him.

"Yeah, I'm not sure how I'll ever be able to apologize enough for my… let's call it anger issues, when you saw me in there."

"In where?" I asked, wanting to understand exactly what had happened.

It was wonderful that I had my Hayden back, but I needed to know how he came to be my Hayden. I didn't think it was common for coma patients and their doctors to somehow connect on a psychic level.

"I promise I'll explain everything to you later, but right now I've got to be a good doctor and tell you to go back to sleep. You really need your rest," he said, still sounding too nice and throwing me off a bit.

"You're not… my mother," I said sarcastically.

"Apparently you responded better to the jerky version of myself," he said, still smiling down at me.

I tried to shrug my shoulders but it proved too difficult so instead I just started up at him challengingly, ecstatic to be having this familiar little exchange with him.

"I know your slow Southern mentality makes it difficult for you to follow directions, but go to bed right now and try not to screw it up somehow," he deadpanned.

"That's… more like it."

CHAPTER 24

I was convinced Hayden must have snuck something into my IV before he left, because I actually slept amazingly well for the rest of the night and by the time I opened my eyes the next morning, my family was in my room again, watching me like a hawk.

"Hi guys," I said wearily, smiling through my sleepiness.

"Isla, you can talk," my mom said tearfully, taking my hand in hers and giving it a little squeeze.

"I'm so sorry about the truck," I instantly said.

I knew this was probably pretty low on the list of conversational topics that day, but I had to say it before I forgot. The truck Daddy had gotten me was expensive and they weren't rich. I'd owned it for less than an hour before completely totaling it.

"Somehow I think you've paid for it enough," Daddy

said to me with a grin. “Don’t worry about that for a second. We’re just glad you’re all right.”

“What happened, Isla?” my brother asked, looking somewhere between excitement to see me again and genuine curiosity. “The police said it looked like you just swerved off the road for no reason.”

“I dropped the CD you got me,” I said, amazed at how easily my speech came now. “And I reached down to get it, but when I looked up there was a dog in the road.”

“You nearly got yourself killed trying to avoid a dog?” my dad asked skeptically.

Surely the daughter of a hunter wouldn’t swerve for a dog.

“Yes Daddy,” I said with a laugh. “It happened really fast. I just panicked.”

“And because you were trying to get the CD, I’m going to guess you’ll try to pin this whole thing on me?” Tuck asked jokingly.

“You know it,” I told him before suddenly getting dizzy again.

I closed my eyes briefly against my sudden lack of balance and waited a moment until the room stopped spinning.

“You all right, baby?” my mom asked, sounding

worried. "Tuck, why don't you go grab the doctor."

My eyes snapped open instantly at the thought that I'd be seeing Hayden again in the same room as my family. It was like having two different lives that were suddenly crashing together. It had been weird enough when I'd first woken up, but now that I knew Hayden knew me and what we'd experienced was somehow real, it was just too weird.

Almost immediately, a man in scrubs walked into the room and checked my IVs and machines, examining me closely.

"She may experience some dizziness for a while. We'll get her into physical therapy once she's up and moving again to work on her balance and make sure her neck has full range of motion," the doctor informed my family.

"Where's Hayden?" I asked in confusion.

"Hayden?" my mom replied, looking down at me like she was worried I was seeing things.

"Dr. Temple is off at the moment, but he should return later tonight," the other doctor said, nodding to my parents and leaving the room.

"Hayden?" my mom asked me again.

"Dr. Temple," I mumbled, my cheeks flushing.

"Uh oh," Tuck said with a wicked grin on his face.

"Well, someone's got to provide for her, son. She got a

degree in vocal performance," my dad said, always eager to tease me about my major. "She might as well fall for a doctor if she wants any hope of living in a home that isn't on wheels."

It was like I hadn't been gone at all. They were already right back to teasing me.

"My head feels a lot better," I said loudly, hoping I could change the subject, even though I was happy that my family wasn't the sad, mourning type.

Even if they drove me nuts, I was glad that they weren't treating me any differently. I could use some normalcy right at that moment.

"Probably all thanks to *Hayden*," my brother stated, very unhelpfully.

"Gee, I'm super tired guys," I lied, yawning for effect.

Yes, I was excited to see my family again and yes, I was happy to not be dead, but there was no way I was going to talk about my crush on my doctor with Tuck. I'd rather play the recovering-coma-patient card first.

"We'll let you rest, honey," my mom said sweetly.

"She's totally faking it, Mom," Tuck pointed out, though it was in vain. My parents were already hurrying him out the door.

"Love you guys!" I called after them, mentally shaking

my head at my brother.

He was completely impossible.

~~~

"Knock, knock," Hayden called, poking his head in the door before coming in.

He must have been off the clock because he wore white Chuck Taylors, fitted khaki pants, and a light blue shirt that brought out his distractingly blue eyes.

"What are you doing here?" I asked in confusion, glad that I was finally sitting up in bed so that we didn't have to have another awkward conversation with me lying down. And also extremely glad that the hospital had let me brush my teeth.

"It's nice to see you too," he said sarcastically.

Maybe his personality wasn't as exaggerated as he let on. Though I had to admit that he was still much nicer than he ever was in the tasks.

"Sorry I just… the other doctor said you didn't work until later tonight."

"I don't," he confirmed, coming to sit by my bed. "But I thought I should bring you something to say sorry for… you know… throwing you off a cliff and yelling at you… a
~~~

lot."

He pulled a small bouquet of white lilies from behind his back and offered them to me. I took them from him but raised my eyebrow at the gesture.

"Aren't these funeral flowers?" I asked.

"I couldn't resist," he said with a grin. "You just kept going on and on about how you were dead, so it seemed appropriate."

Yep. He was my Hayden after all. Just my Hayden mixed with a nice person.

"So you knew I wasn't dead the whole time?" I asked incredulously, wondering how he could let me think I'd lost my family forever.

"Technically I knew," he said guiltily. "But I didn't know when I was with you."

"Okay, you're seriously going to have to explain to me what happened, because I'm way past confused."

"It's pretty intense… are you ready to run this particular mental gauntlet?" he asked, sounding like the Hayden I knew, who had no faith in me.

"Glad to see your personality hasn't changed *that* much," I accused, narrowing my eyes at him.

He ignored my statement and went on as if I'd never spoken.

Typical.

"When the ambulance brought you here, it was pretty obvious you'd had some major head trauma," he began, placing his hand on the bed just inches away from mine.

I resisted the urge to take his hand and opted for listening to his explanation of my bizarre experience with him instead.

"You were unconscious but had full brain function. You were breathing on your own, your brain was sending all the right signals to keep you alive, but you wouldn't wake up. We were sure the head trauma had caused the coma, we just weren't sure how to bring you back out of it."

I imagined how scary the whole thing must have been for my parents and instantly regretted ever going down that mental road. It was too painful.

"We've had cases like this before and we'd been developing a new procedure to help guide our coma patients back into consciousness, but it was extremely untested. We'd only tried it once before."

"On your cousin?" I asked, remembering Hayden's regret over her. He nodded somberly, looking away from me. "What happened to her?"

"I tried the same thing we tried with you but… it didn't

work. We never got her back."

I shuddered at the thought and, despite my reservations, grabbed Hayden's hand and gave it a squeeze. He looked up at me and gave me a sad smile before regaining his composure and going on.

"Your parents were reluctant to try it but after you didn't wake up for a few days with no signs of improvement, they decided to give it a shot."

"It's a new procedure?" I asked, to which Hayden nodded. "It must be expensive."

When I'd been with Hayden in the tasks, I'd expressed my hope that I was, in fact, dead, because sitting in a hospital meant I was taking the most expensive nap ever. Now that I was alive and awake, I'd have to live with the financial ruin I'd brought on my family.

The thought made me sick to my stomach.

"My parents can't afford something like that," I said with a heavy sigh.

"I remember you mentioning that when I was with you once… or twice… or a million times, so I took the liberty of setting up a fund in your name here at the hospital," he said, and suddenly, I was grateful that he wasn't as mean as he'd been in the tasks. "People must love your family because we raised more than enough to cover your hospital costs. In fact, people were really eager to rally around your family. You're something of a local icon now."

"Great. The girl who almost died trying not to hit a dog is an icon," I said sarcastically, though I was, in fact, incredibly grateful.

I wasn't sure I'd ever be able to repay the generosity of the strangers who'd donated so much time and money to keep my family afloat. It made my eyes burn a bit with the tears I wouldn't allow myself to shed in front of Hayden.

I'd wait until he left.

"Thank you for doing that, Hayden," I said seriously, hoping he understood just how much he'd saved my family. "I know you don't like it when I'm all mushy, but you really did us a huge favor. I don't think you understand just how much you helped my parents out."

"I don't hate emotion *that* much, Isla. I told you, I'm not nearly as heartless as you think I am."

I wasn't sure I believed him just yet, but his actions were definitely starting to change my opinion of him. It seemed like no matter what, I never quite knew what to make of Hayden. For better or worse, he always surprised me.

"So, the procedure?" I asked, trying to get the conversation back on track.

"Right," he said, shaking his head to focus once more. "It sounds a little science fiction-y, but we've developed an experimental procedure where we pretty much link our brains with a series of wires and transmitters."

I gave him an odd look at this description. It didn't sound like a real thing.

"I know… that's why it's experimental," he said, realizing how crazy his explanation sounded. "They'd hook us up together, put me under, and ease me into your mind with a serum we're working on. And if that isn't impossible enough for you, all of those 'tasks' you were performing… do you want to guess what those were?"

"Some sick, sadistic, thing you thought up to torture me?" I ventured.

"Close, but no," he said, giving me a look for my sarcastic answer. "You and I were actually mapping different parts of your brain, trying to regain function in each area. So you'd conquer a memory task and--."

"I'd have control over my own memory again," I finished, sounding distant.

It was crazy, and completely far-fetched, but somehow it still made sense. No matter how unbelievable Hayden's explanation was, they'd tried it and it had worked, so by some miracle, the whole thing was possible.

"So failing a task meant… what?" I asked.

"You failed to regain control over that part of your brain; and unless you had full use of these different areas in your mind, you wouldn't be waking up from the coma," he explained. "That's why it was so important you didn't fail the tasks."

"Then why didn't you just say that in the first place?" I asked incredulously, my accent thicker now that I was so emotional. "I wouldn't have been such a pain if I actually understood what was going on."

"Would you calm down and let me explain, you mad woman?" he asked, giving me a look that strongly reminded me of our time together in the cycles.

It was a look that said, "You are so incredibly annoying."

"Because the procedure was experimental there were still a lot of bugs to work out. One of the biggest being that I couldn't differentiate reality from what was in your mind when I was with you."

"That seems like a *big* bug," I said.

"Tell me about it. I'd be here with your family, telling them we're making all sorts of progress and really hopeful that I'd be able to help you, then I'd go into this weird space where the only memory I possessed was this vague idea that I was your Guide and had to get you to your Destination. That's all I knew."

"Not to mention all of my memories you had access to," I pointed out.

"That was just another odd side effect," he said dismissively. "But imagine my frustration when I'd come back out of that space and into the real world? I was so angry that I couldn't ever remember to tell you what was really going on and I'd hate myself for being so rude to you but there wasn't a whole lot I could do about it. I always tried to tell myself I'd explain everything to you the second I went back in, but I'd forget almost immediately."

"Yeah, something tells me this procedure would have gone a lot smoother if you'd been nice and could tell me that I wasn't dead."

"Just a bit smoother," he joked, looking down at me with a grin that heated my cheeks up.

"So what was with the bizarre weather in each cycle?" I asked. "Or was that just my crazy imagination?"

"I'm not positive, but I have a theory," he began.

"Which is?"

"It was always sunny before I came into the cycle right?"

"Right," I confirmed.

"Well I always checked your pupils before going under and connecting to your mind. I'm kind of wondering if the 'sun' you saw, was actually just my flashlight."

"That would make sense," I said slowly. "But it doesn't explain the fog or the snow."

"More theories," he replied with a grin.

"This should be good."

"The fog was probably from the serum we had to pump through your IV when they connected us to each other. It always made my mind a little hazy so maybe that translated into fog for you?"

"Doesn't sound as convincing as the sun theory, but go on," I teased.

"The snow was probably the same thing. As the serum leaves your system it leaves behind a cold sensation in your veins, so every time the serum ran out and the cycle came to a close, you rationalized the cold in your veins with snow that made you sleep."

"So I really do just have an odd imagination."

"Or a brilliant one. You definitely came up with creative ways to explain everything that was happening to you," he said, sounding almost impressed.

"I'm nothing if not creative," I agreed. "So each cycle was on a set amount of time? It seemed like the completion of a cycle depended on how quickly I got through each task."

"I think we were lucky the timing worked out that way, but it was definitely on a timed basis."

"But I felt like the cycles got longer towards the end there."

Hayden looked down at the floor guiltily.

"What?" I asked, trying to coax his secret out of him.

"I may or may not have told your family I'd need more time with you for the later tasks," he admitted.

"But you didn't?" I asked, thinking that seemed like a true statement.

The longer the tasks had gone on, the more difficult they had become. It only made sense that he'd need more time with me to make sure I'd completed them all.

"Not really. I just wanted to spend more time with you. You know… when you were alive and vibrant and not unconscious in a hospital bed." He swallowed uncomfortably at this revelation. It was pretty obvious he wasn't all that in to expressing his feelings. "Of course I didn't realize that's why the cycles were longer once I got in there, since I forgot any and all valuable information right when they put me under."

He sounded put out by this fact, but his smile that

seemed so quick to return told me otherwise.

I liked the smiley Hayden.

"Plus you can imagine how embarrassing it was for me to kiss you… in your mind that is, and then wake up in a room with your parents. Not exactly a great way to experience your first kiss with someone."

At the mention of our kiss my heart instantly accelerated and I cursed the stupid machine that was keeping track of my heart rate. Hayden glanced at the rapidly beeping machine but didn't say anything.

"I guess technically we haven't kissed yet, have we?" he asked me, raising his eyebrow at me like he always did, and making my mind much fuzzier than it had been when I'd first woken up from my coma.

"I don't know that it's really all that fair to be having this conversation while I'm hooked up to this machine," I protested, unable to ignore the persistent beeping that wouldn't seem to slow down while Hayden was in the room.

He leaned in a bit closer to me and placed his hand over mine, tapping on the small rubber clamp that rested over my finger.

"What, this?" he asked, his voice incredibly deep and soft.

The machine sped up a few beats.

"Yes that," I answered in practiced annoyance.

He was so close now, his smile never faltering, and the beeping on my machine growing ever faster.

"I kind of like it," he whispered, slipping the receiver off of my finger and closing the space between us.

The kiss wasn't deep like our first (imagined?) one was. Instead he gently pressed his lips to mine for just a few seconds before pulling away again, his scruffy five o'clock shadow tickling my skin.

"That was highly unprofessional," I joked quietly, nudging his nose with my own.

"I'm kind of a lousy doctor," he agreed, leaning in again and giving me another slow, long kiss.

He still smelled like soap and his long fingers gently trailed down the inside of my arm to my wrist before he ended the kiss and stood back up.

"And I'm supposed to be letting you rest."

"What?" I asked, incredulously. "Hayden Temple, you can't just kiss me then walk away. You sit your butt back down this instant and finish explaining everything to me or I'll be pushing *you* off of a cliff the next chance I get. The door swings both ways."

"Glad I didn't just imagine your stubbornness," he said

with a long-suffering sigh, still moving towards the door and wordlessly informing me I had lost that battle; I had to sleep whether I wanted to or not.

"You haven't won, you know," I told him smugly. "I've got a lot more questions and I know where you work."

"Luckily, we have more than enough time together," he said, acting like this fact was a burden to him. "Probably too much time."

"Just as long as our time together doesn't involve any more tasks," I stated with a grin. "Or else I might have to sit back and watch while you try to complete impossible and completely nonsensical tasks while I just pop in and out whenever I please. Sound familiar?"

"You don't have the patience," he challenged.

"Oh Hayden, you're going to have so much fun learning about my lack of patience."

"I don't know what I've gotten myself into with you, but I can see you're going to be a handful," he said in mock exasperation as he gave me one last sideways smirk and walked out the door.

He had no idea.

Acknowledgments

These acknowledgments are going to be weird. I mean, weirder than normal, because this book was such an odd one to write. Thank you to Dr. Ice and Dr. Okinawa for all of the "facts" you gave me. Because goodness knows if there's one thing I hate, it's trying to figure out facts when all I want is to be creative. If I got anything wrong, now the blame is on you. Just kidding. But really. Ashlee, thank you for fangirling with me over these characters to get me even more excited about this book. Zack Snyder, I've only seen one of your movies, but it was the best thing ever. And it made me want to write some crazy stuff, which is exactly what I did in this book. Killian and Scarlett, in a very not subtle way, thank you for being perfect. Mumford and Sons, I'm sorry I said you killed my heroine, but I guess that just proves how great your music is. Family, thank you, as usual, for putting up with me. Especially since I couldn't stop saying "Isn't Isla stubborn? Aren't they funny together? Isn't Hayden cute?" about fictional characters that I wrote. Probably not healthy. Jackie, thank you for the clay and the candy and being so Sherlock-y and for editing and cover designing and filming creepy movies with me. Husband, thank you for brainstorming with me and being the most wonderful person in the universe. Hemingway, thank you for not eating any rough drafts of this book. And to my Father in Heaven, thank you for this gift.

TURN THE PAGE FOR A SNEAK PEEK AT THE SEQUEL TO UNDER ZENITH!

Beyond Lyra

CHAPTER 1

Thirty-five miles per hour.

Thirty-five.

Why on earth were there even roads where the speed limit was only thirty-five miles per hour? I wasn't sure there was ever a time when a car would need to travel that slowly. Of course I wouldn't dare go above the speed limit since the last time I'd done that I'd gotten into a car accident that landed me in a three-week coma. But still. Thirty-five miles per hour? Seriously?

I glanced at the clock on the dashboard of my very junky car and tapped my thumb quickly against the steering wheel. It was bad enough that I looked like an old pile of laundry because I'd gotten ready so quickly, but now I was going to be late for work and there was nothing I could do about it.

Somehow, it had completely slipped my mind that I had a shift at *Andie's* that night. The only reason I was currently (not) speeding down the road to the local bar and grill, was because my roommate Monica had called asking why I wasn't at work to relieve her shift.

Now I was stuck with a pile of messy hair and half applied makeup as I pulled into work. I jumped out of my car, straightening my full white skirt and tucking in my short-sleeved, white, collared shirt as I ran into the little bar in the quickly fading daylight.

"Where have you been?" Monica whispered as I clocked in, pulling my long, wavy, white-blonde hair into a messy low side bun. "You were supposed to be here thirty minutes ago."

"I'm sorry," I said emphatically, hoping she didn't hate me too much.

She was, after all, my best friend.

She'd threatened numerous times to move back to New York after we'd both graduated from East Carolina University almost a year ago, but something had kept her in North Carolina. She said it was our undying friendship, but I got the feeling it had more to do with my brother Tucker, who was sitting at the bar shooting glances at her. Right in front of me.

"Are you okay?" Monica asked seriously, stopping me as I began tying my apron.

"Yeah, why?" I asked, hoping she wasn't talking about the only taboo topic of conversation that I'd avoided exploring for an entire month.

"You've been really forgetful lately. It's not like you," she said, relieving me to no end.

I had been worried she was talking about--.

"Oh great," Monica said, rolling her eyes as she looked over my shoulder.

My stomach sank. I knew what she was looking at without even having to check.

"Let me guess. Brunette?" I said with a long-suffering sigh, suddenly wishing I'd actually done my makeup well today.

"As usual," she answered.

I took a deep breath, drawing strength from the hate Monica and I fed, before turning around and briefly meeting eyes with the most beautiful man in the world.

Of course he was also the most awful man, so the moment was slightly lessened.

Dr. Hayden Temple stood near the entrance to *Andie's* in all of his terrible, beautiful, glory, scoping out a table in my section and making me want to duck behind the bar and never show my face again.

He gave me his classic sideways smirk, making his gorgeous blue eyes squint before ruffling his dark hair and turning his attention back to the sexy brunette on his arm.

They were always brunette.

Somehow I thought it was Hayden's favorite way of driving the nail into the coffin of our dead relationship.

He wore the light blue, long-sleeved Henley shirt I had gotten him for his birthday and a pair of jeans. Much more buttoned down and relaxed than he normally looked.

The brunette whispered something into his ear, tracing her fingers over his chest as she did so. His lips tugged up in the corners and for the briefest of moments, his eyes flicked up to me before the pair proceeded to their booth, which happened to be conveniently located in my section.

He always sat in my section on his "dates".

"I don't have to go home. I can take your table," Monica offered as Tuck joined us by the side of the bar, looking furious.

He had taken our breakup particularly hard since he'd finally gotten a "brother" rather than the dress-wearing sister he had always been stuck with. Now any time he saw Hayden, he shot him dirty looks and plotted ways to get back at him for the demise of our relationship. It didn't really help that for some reason, Hayden felt the need to bring every girl in town to my section at *Andie's* almost every night.

I knew for a fact that he could cook. He didn't need me to wait on him and his floozies.

"I'll even spill a pitcher of beer on him," Monica added, sounding a little too pleased with that thought.

"I'm fine," I lied, even as I squinted against a headache that had begun to form.

It didn't really surprise me that Hayden had brought a headache with him.

"This is ridiculous, Isla. You shouldn't have to wait on that jerk," Tuck said in his thick Southern drawl, being very brotherly all of a sudden. "I'm gonna go talk to him."

"Don't you dare Tucker Edison, that would be completely mortifying," I said quickly, putting a stop to my brother's mutinous thoughts. "I'm a big girl. I can handle one silly little ex-boyfriend without calling in backup," I assured him and Monica.

They both looked skeptical but I wasn't ready for more protests from them, so I cut them off by plastering a fake smile onto my face, grabbing my note pad, and walking over to one of my other tables first.

I may have been tough, but I needed a minute or two to

regain my composure before facing Hayden and The Girl.

Monica rolled her eyes but both she and Tuck walked towards the exit, apparently trusting me enough to let me handle this on my own.

"Hi there. I'm Isla and I'll be your server today," I said to the friendly-looking couple who had just sat down in my section at the table right across from Hayden's booth. "Can I get y'all something to drink to start off with?"

"I'd like something to drink," Hayden's deep voice said behind me, his English accent always giving me chills despite my best efforts to ignore him.

I never let my smile falter, no matter how fake it was. Instead I turned to look at him, still beaming, and kept my voice incredibly even.

"Why don't you just hold that thought and I'll be with you in just one moment, sir," I told him, proud of just how normal I could be around him.

"We'll just have water," the man said, barely glancing at me as he perused the menu. I had no more excuses to avoid Hayden.

Taking a deep breath and locking my smile firmly in place, I turned on the heel of my cowboy boots to face Hayden and The Girl, looking them both in the eyes and refusing to back down.

"Welcome to *Andie's.* My name is Isla, and I'll be your server today," I recited, trying to forget about how I'd told Hayden that my Daddy joked I'd end up a waitress, even with my "fancy degree". "Can I start you off with some drinks?"

Hayden kept his icy blue eyes fixed on me, the sideways smirk never leaving his face. He looked like a cat who had caught a mouse. It was unsettling to say the least.

"What would you like, Love?" he asked the girl sitting across from him without ever looking at her.

Of course it didn't escape my notice that he'd called her "Love". Something he always used to call me.

Maybe it was just a British thing. Not a term of endearment?

"I'll just take some white wine, sweetie" the girl said to me condescendingly, looking at me over her shoulder and giggling for effect.

No matter how crazy it made me that Hayden insisted on brining a different girl to the restaurant every night, I at least got some petty pleasure over the caliber of women he had begun dating since our breakup. I may not have been some smart, rich doctor like Hayden, but at least I wasn't a vapid twelve-year-old.

"Right away, *sweetie*," I repeated, trying to hide my

grin as I turned to leave, obviously making Hayden mad that he hadn't gotten to me.

Unfortunately, he reached out and grabbed my arm, forcing me to stay at his table before I could make my great escape.

"You forgot to take my order, Love," he said with a fake pout, using the "L" word again.

He really seemed to love that word today.

"So sorry about that, Doctor Temple," I answered with a sweet smile, pretending to mock him even as I racked my brain trying to remember if I really had taken his drink order already and he was just messing with me.

I could have sworn I had taken it.

He let his fingers trail down my arm almost imperceptibly as he dropped his hand from me and looked down at his menu.

"You know what, I'm driving tonight. I'll just have water," he finally finished, making me wonder why I had wasted my time taking his "order" at all.

"Perfect," I said too brightly. This game was quickly losing its appeal. "I'll get those drinks and be right back to take your order. Did you want a kid's menu for her?" I added with a smirk at Hayden, finally saying something that fazed him.

He narrowed his eyes at me while still keeping his smile in place.

"We're fine," he said evenly.

I resisted the urge to light his hair on fire with the candle on the table and instead walked away from the couple, feeling triumphant with my performance.

I could feel Hayden's eyes watching me as I made my way back into the kitchen, placing the drink order in front of our chef and heading to the bathroom to try to save some face. If I had to wait on my infuriating ex-boyfriend and his beautiful date, I could at least put some lipstick on.

"Isla?" our cook Matt called just before I reached the bathroom.

"Yeah?" I called back, trying to remember why I was heading towards the bathroom in the first place.

"This order is just drinks," he began slowly, looking at me like I had five heads. "Did you hand me the wrong paper?"

I took the paper in question from his hands and scanned it skeptically.

"Oh," I said, unable to believe I'd really given him an order for just drinks when I normally got those myself. "Yeah, sorry about that. I don't know what I was thinking."

"Must be on auto-pilot," he suggested with a warm

smile.

"Yeah."

"Probably that good-for-nothing ex-boyfriend of yours," he went on knowingly. "You just say the word and I'll add a few walnuts to his food. He's allergic, right?"

"Thanks Matty," I said with a laugh, pocketing the drink order and suddenly remembering why I needed to go to the bathroom. "I think I'll be fine without you poisoning him. Besides, if anyone gets to do that, it'll be me."

"Hang in there," he said as he turned to leave.

He was a good friend.

I looked down at my hand on the bathroom doorknob and paused for a moment, trying to gather my thoughts and figure out why I was standing there. I knew it had something to do with Hayden, but I couldn't quite figure out what it was.

Glancing up at Hayden's table, I caught him glaring daggers at Matt as he walked back to the kitchen to continue working. I shook my head at his crazy behavior and tried to ignore him so I could figure out my own mess of a memory at that moment.

Why was I standing by the bathroom?

"Lipstick," I whispered to myself with a smile.

I was going to put some lipstick on so that I didn't look

like such a train wreck.

How could I have possibly forgotten that so quickly?

Walking into the dimly lit bathroom, I pulled a rosy lip gloss from the pocket of my apron and applied it in earnest, figuring it was probably the only thing that could salvage this night. I didn't look *terrible*, but I had been so tired lately that I'd just fall asleep randomly throughout the day, making me look groggy all the time. Today, unfortunately, was no exception.

"This will be a fun night," I told my reflection sarcastically as my phone buzzed in my pocket.

Technically I wasn't supposed to have it on me at work, but I was always worried that something might happen to my parents or my brother the one day I left it in my purse and I'd miss the call to come to the hospital.

That car accident had made me completely paranoid.

"Tuck?" I said questioningly to my text message, wondering what he could possibly need from me when he knew I was at work.

What's the code to Hayden's car? The message read, and while that sentence should have set off some major alarm bells in my head, for some reason I simply answered him without thinking then slipped my phone back into my apron before leaving the bathroom to face Hayden once more.

"I got your drinks together for you," Matt said when I entered the kitchen.

He gave me the same worried look Monica had given me earlier, but I hardly noticed.

"How should I do this?" I asked him.

"Face Hayden?"

"No," I said dismissively. "Well… yes. But I mean, the drinks. Should I bring them out and then get the food orders from both tables? Or only bring one of my tables their drinks, take their orders, leave to get the drinks from my other table, and then…," I let my words trail off.

How had I dealt with two tables at once before? Why could I suddenly not make a decision about anything in my life? Did Hayden really have that big of an effect on me?

"Isla, are you feeling all right?" Matt asked me.

"Yeah, I'm just having some issues strategizing," I said with a laugh. "It's no big deal, I'll just play it by ear while I try to figure out a way to get back at him," I assured him with a chipper smile, picking up the tray full of drinks and making my way back to my tables.

Hayden's date was talking to him, though he hardly seemed to notice. Instead he was watching me with the same scowl he'd thrown Matt's way.

Matt and I were far from having a romantic relationship, but the way Hayden was icily watching the two of us made me wonder if he thought I'd finally moved on. Really, it wasn't any of his business either way, since he had been the one to dump me.

Still, I sort of hoped he cared about my current relationship status, no matter how nonexistent it was.

"Here are your waters," I said to my first table. "And I'll give you another minute or two to look over the menu."

I gave them a peppy smile before turning to face Hayden again.

"Here are your drinks, Doctor Temple," I singsonged, knowing he *hated* it when I called him that. "I'll be right back to take your food order."

"Oh I think we're ready now," He said, stopping me once more before I could leave.

"Fantastic, *Doctor Temple*," I intoned, with as much sweet sarcasm as I possibly could.

His lips tightened just a fraction as his frustration grew, but if there was one thing I knew about him, it was that he wasn't a fan of outright confrontation. He'd take thinly veiled criticisms over a fight any day.

"Hey Sophie," Hayden said, getting his date's attention. "You know Isla used to be a singer?"

"Great," his date said, with about as much enthusiasm as a depressed undertaker.

Apparently she *had* caught he "kid's menu" remark.

"Or are you still doing that?" he asked, feigning interest when I knew he was just setting up some awful rude comment. "I mean, waiting tables must take up a lot of your time and energy. I can't imagine you can really pursue two passions at once, can you?"

I flexed my fingers that were hidden beneath my drink tray, wanting desperately to punch him in his beautiful face. Luckily, I had some sense of will power and refrained, since that would definitely get me fired in a heartbeat.

Maybe I *would* let Matt put walnuts in Hayden's meal.

"Did you know what you wanted to order?" I asked, wishing more than anything that I could think up a good comeback, but with my heart pounding in my ears from my anger, my reasoning under pressure wasn't quite working.

Of course that made me sound like I was back in the stupid tests that had brought Hayden and me together in the first place. "Reasoning under pressure". What a joke. Although I'd pay a lot of money to have Hayden unconscious again like he had been in that task.

If I hadn't ever gotten into that car accident, I never

would have fallen into a coma, and Hayden never would have broken into my mind to guide me through those useless tasks, and we never would have met. I would have been perfectly content and not having a mild panic attack right at that moment.

Dr. Hayden Temple was actually a brilliant brain surgeon. He'd invented his own unorthodox, and unfortunately only-sometimes-successful procedure to help coma patients regain control over their own minds by conquering things one trait at a time: agility, motor skills, reasoning under pressure, ingenuity, strategy, and memory. I was sure there was actually a deeper and more complex way of describing the parts of my brain we mapped, but that was about what it boiled down to.

Of course he'd only ever tried the procedure on me and his cousin.

It had worked for me.

His cousin was another story. One we didn't talk about.

The only problem with Hayden's brilliant procedure, was that the two of us seemed to have amnesia during our time mapping my brain. I'd had no idea that I was in a coma and spent my entire time in the cycles thinking I was dead and trying to get to heaven. And Hayden, brilliant as he was, would be put under in the hospital every day, wake up inside of my mind, and totally forget that he was a doctor trying to help a coma patient back to consciousness. Instead, he thought he was some jerky, self-righteous, all-knowing Guide who was supposed to shepherd his charge to an unknown goal.

I mean, I guess technically he was right, but knowing I was in a coma would have made the entire process so much smoother.

He still had some kinks to work out with his procedure.

Although no matter how terrible the experience of battling through my own mind with Hayden had been, I had one thing to be grateful to him for. I was alive. And without him I wouldn't be.

"I'll just have a chicken salad," The Girl said, now openly glaring at me for the attention her date was giving me.

"That sounds like an excellent choice, Sophie," Hayden told her in what I'm sure was supposed to be an appreciative tone.

Instead he just sounded condescending. As usual.

"I'll have the same."

"I'll be right back with that," I told him, the fake smile still in place.

I kept it plastered to my lips as I made my way back to the kitchen, knowing that Hayden was *still* watching me. The guy really needed to find a new hobby other than bringing his dates to my place of work to torture me endlessly. It was getting old.

"How're you holding up, kid?" Matt asked, looking over the paper I had given him.

"Ugh. Matty, can you please just get him run out of town for me?"

"I know a guy," he assured me with a sly wink. "I'll get these salads put together right now so you can get him out of here as quickly as possible."

"You're an angel," I emphasized, leaning my head against the cool wall and closing my eyes. "Of course I'd have a headache on top of everything else."

"Did you get your other table's order already? I might as well just do both while you're here," Matt suggested.

"I totally forgot to get theirs," I groaned. "They're probably going to be mad about the wait."

"Give them some complementary chips and queso and I'm sure they won't care," he said, putting the two salads, chips, and queso onto my tray for me.

Normally he didn't have to babysit me so much while I waited tables, but my mind didn't seem to be working tonight and Matt had taken notice.

"You're sure you don't want to call it an early night and go home? You look beat."

"Always complementing me, Matty," I answered sarcastically, taking my tray and exiting the kitchen.

I weaved between tables with the tray balanced precariously on my palm, trying not to look at Hayden as I brought his food over.

I was only about three steps from him when one of the seated guests scooted their chair back to get up, hitting me in the hip and making me lose my balance. As desperately as I tried, I couldn't seem to regain my footing and as I lurched forward and propelled a tray filled with food at Hayden and his date, I took a moment to wonder how I could possibly be this unlucky.

ABOUT THE AUTHOR

Shannen Crane Camp was born and raised in Southern California, where she developed a love of reading, writing, and anything having to do with film. After high school, she moved to Utah to attend Brigham Young University, where she received a degree in Media Arts and found herself a husband in fellow California native Josh Camp. The two now live in Utah with their miniature schnauzer Hemingway. Shannen's true love is Young Adult Fiction though she often dabbles in New Adult, Paranormal, and Mystery. She takes any opportunity to include her love of film and video games in her writing and you might just find a nerdy Easter Egg or two hidden in her works.

Shannen loves to hear from readers, so feel free to contact her at Shannencbooks@hotmail.com or visit her website for more information: http://shannencbooks.blogspot.com